ROBOT RACERS

BOOK 2

Robot Racers is published in the United States by
Stone Arch Books, A Capstone Imprint
1710 Roe Crest Drive
North Mankato, Minnesota 56003
www.capstonepub.com

First published in 2013 by Curious Fox,
an imprint of Capstone Global Library Limited
7 Pilgrim Street, London, EC4V 6LB
Registered company number: 6695582
www.curious-fox.com

Text © Hothouse Fiction Ltd 2013
Series created by Hothouse Fiction
www.hothousefiction.com
The author's moral rights are hereby asserted.

Library of Congress Cataloging-in-Publication Data is available on the
Library of Congress website.

ISBN: 978-1-4342-6571-5 (hardcover)
ISBN: 978-1-4342-7937-8 (paperback)

Summary: Jimmy and his robot, Maverick, were thrilled to qualify for Robot
Races. After finishing second in the first race, they're out to win the next
challenge, in the Amazon rain forest. But Jimmy's enemy Horace has other
ideas.

Artistic Elements: Shutterstock

Designer: Alison Thiele

With special thanks to David Grant

Printed in China.
092013   007740LEOS14

BY AXEL LEWIS

STONE ARCH BOOKS™
a capstone imprint   www.capstonepub.com

TABLE OF CONTENTS

CHAPTER 1
HIGHLIGHTS AND HEROES

"Come on, Maverick! You can do it!" shouted Jimmy at the top of his lungs. Maverick squealed around a corner. His back end swerved away from the winding road. He was going so fast he nearly toppled over the side of the narrow track into the deep canyon below. The wheels spun as the robot racer tried to speed off, sending a cloud of dust up into the air.

"Look at that! That is the smartest bit of driving I've seen in years!" said the American commentator on the TV.

Jimmy smiled proudly. "Watch your speed, Maverick!" he shouted at the old television.

Of course, he had no reason to worry. He knew exactly what would happen next in the race because he had been driving Maverick at the time.

Jimmy and his best friend, Max, were sitting on the old sofa in Jimmy's living room. They were watching a rerun of the first stage of the Robot Races Championship. On the screen, the cloud of dust and exhaust settled to show Maverick racing along the sandy track, a heat haze rising in front of him. The camera rose to show the other contestants at different points in the race.

There was Princess Kako in her silver outfit, riding her robobike, Lightning. She looked effortlessly cool as she zipped along the track.

Chip, the American racer, was in his large yellow digger-like robot called Dug. The size and weight of Dug meant that he didn't look as elegant as Princess Kako.

Then there was Samir. In his deadly-looking hoverbot, Maximus, Samir quietly swept by competitors.

Missy, the Australian tomboy, trundled along in her four-wheeled giant racer, Monster. Missy and Monster were tough.

Finally the camera panned to show the sleek black robot named Zoom. Jimmy winced as the camera turned to its driver, Horace Pelly. Horace had been annoying enough when Jimmy was at school with him. But now that they were racing against each other, and he had hit new levels of smugness. Jimmy couldn't believe it when Horace flipped the visor up on his helmet and winked at the camera.

Jimmy rolled his eyes at Horace. *What a show- off,* he thought.

On the TV, the racers were coming to the final section of the track. Jimmy allowed himself to grin. After all, he knew how the race ended!

"This is shaping up to be one of the most exciting finishes of a Robot Race ever!" yelled the TV commentator.

"Go, Maverick, go!" Max whooped in the living room, bouncing up and down on the sofa. He really was the best friend a guy could ask for.

Jimmy watched the TV closely. He saw himself and Maverick closing in on the two state-of-the-art robots, Lightning and Zoom.

Jimmy had been watching the Robot Races for years. He still couldn't believe that he was actually taking part in them. Even though he knew how it all turned out, he couldn't help feeling nervous. With the finish line in sight, Princess Kako had opened up a gap between herself and the other two racers, leaving Jimmy and Horace battling it out for second place.

"Fire your rocket-boosters!" Max shouted at the TV, and Jimmy grinned. It was so strange to hear his best friend cheering him on in the same way that they'd always cheered for their favorite robot racers.

On the screen, the other Jimmy held his nerve, waiting until the last moment to use his boosters. With the checkered flag in the air up ahead, there was an explosion of fire from Maverick's thrusters. The rockets propelled him across the line into second place.

"Yes!" yelled Jimmy.

"Awesome!" shrieked Max.

They jumped in the air and high-fived before doing a little dance together in the middle of the room. Jimmy immediately felt a bit silly celebrating a finish that had taken place over a week ago, but the rerun was the first chance he'd had to see the race since he'd taken part in it. The TV cut to the commentators in the studio.

"Well, it doesn't get more exciting than that! Princess Kako rockets into first place, while underdog Jimmy Roberts from —" The presenter paused while he tried to say the name of Jimmy's town. "— Smed-ing-ham in the UK, takes second. A fine performance, and we're not the only ones who think so!"

The TV cut to a familiar face. Big Al, one of the superstars of Robot Races, stood alongside his robot, Crusher. He was Jimmy and Max's favorite racer. Jimmy had posters of Big Al all over his bedroom. Max was an even bigger fan. He had once asked his mom if he could get a tattoo of Crusher.

"Big Al, when it was announced that Lord Leadpipe was going to run the Robot Races Championship for children under sixteen years old, did you ever think the talent would be this good?" the interviewer asked.

The large American racer laughed a big, booming laugh. It shook Jimmy's old TV so hard that the picture frame on top of it slid off and crashed to the floor.

"We all know that Lord Leadpipe likes to shake things up. He's a smart guy. He knew what he was doing! The racing I've seen from these youngsters has been crazy, man! That first race was amazing!" Big Al said.

"Who stood out for you?" asked the interviewer.

Big Al turned to look at the camera. "Folks, you only need to remember one name in this competition, and that's Jimmy Roberts."

Jimmy's mouth fell open as he heard his name being mentioned by one of his heroes.

"Jimmy's got it all! Speed, style, and timing. His racing last week was outstanding!"

At home, Jimmy could barely breathe. He was in total shock!

"The robots this year are great," continued Big Al. "There are some cool designs out there, but Maverick is the one to watch. He reminds me of Crusher years ago when I first built him. He doesn't look all that great, but he's got soul."

Max jumped up and down on the sofa in excitement. "Big Al is a fan of my best friend. That practically makes him my friend! Jimmy, do you think he'd take us for a ride in Crusher?"

But Jimmy was too speechless to reply. He felt like he was in a dream. It was just a few weeks since he had first heard of the special Robot Races Championship for kids. And on that very same day he'd learned that his eccentric old grandpa who drove a taxi for a living was actually a robotics genius.

Within days, Grandpa had put together a robot racer made out of his old taxi and some spare parts he had in his shed. The next thing Jimmy knew, he was in the local trials. When he sped to victory, he became a contender for the championship. He was whisked off to the Grand Canyon to compete against the best young racers in the world.

"Well, I guess I better get home," Max said. "Mom wants to take me and my nana shopping."

"Sounds like fun," Jimmy replied, making a face as he opened the front door.

"Not really," said Max. "I'll have to spend an hour watching them choose a pair of socks. It's nowhere near as much fun as hanging around with your grandpa."

Jimmy grinned. Max was right. Living with Grandpa was pretty cool. He watched Max trudge down the street, then went and peered out the back window. At the back of the yard was a rickety old shed with small dirty windows. It looked like the kind of building that you would use for storing a lawn mower and garden tools, but Jimmy knew better.

Jimmy knew that behind those doors lay the entrance to his grandpa's secret underground lab. It had been built by the most secret department of the Secret Services, and it was where Grandpa had built the world's first-ever robot.

The loud banging continued, followed by some horrible grinding and scraping noises. Grandpa had been down there since the previous day, when it had been announced on TV that the next race would be held in South America. The commentators were already calling this stage the rain forest rampage.

As Jimmy looked at the shed, sparks came flying out of the open window. They landed on the uncut grass outside. There was a scary sounding clang and then a roar from inside as the whole shed started to shake.

Jimmy dashed out the back door and ran over to the shed. Putting his hand on the door handle, he braced himself and pulled the door open.

"You okay, Jimmy?" asked Grandpa.

"I'm fine. Are you okay?" Jimmy replied, peering down the slope into the underground lab.

"Why wouldn't I be okay?" Grandpa asked, looking like a crazy scientist with his wild hair and goggles.

There was soot all over his face and oil splattered on his navy-blue overalls. In his hands he held a large silver rocket, which was buzzing dangerously. Before Jimmy could move, a huge jet of blue flame erupted from it, heading straight for him!

CHAPTER 2
UPGRADES AND ADD-ONS

"AAAAHHHH!" cried Jimmy as he felt the heat whoosh toward him. He quickly dived into a nearby bush.

"Whoops!" said Grandpa. "Sorry about that. I'm glad you came over. You're just in time to see the new attachment I've built for Maverick."

"Whoops?" muttered Jimmy, hauling himself out from the bush and patting himself down to make sure nothing was broken.

He put his hands to his face, checking that the heat blast hadn't burned his eyebrows off. Then he pulled a twig from his hair and went into the shed.

Inside, Grandpa was turning dials on the rocket and muttering to himself. Jimmy knew that look. That look meant Grandpa was in full inventor mode.

The gleaming white workshop was filled with hundreds of gadgets and gizmos, which clicked, whirred, steamed, puffed, and fizzed as Grandpa conducted crazy experiments and invented weird and wonderful things. And in the center of the lab sat Grandpa's greatest invention of all — Maverick.

"Hiya, Maverick. You're looking good!" said Jimmy.

Maverick's headlights flashed when he heard Jimmy's voice. "I know! I'm trying out a new car wax. Extra shiny," said the robot in his chirpy voice. "Watch where you're sticking that thing, Grandpa. Don't scratch my paint work!"

Grandpa bent down and started attaching the deadly weapon he had nearly fried Jimmy with to the side of Maverick. The rocket now matched another shiny missile-shaped contraption on the other side.

"It's a nitro-blaster. All those other racers will be making improvements after the last race, so I've had to work hard to upgrade your old boosters. Fire these blasters during the race and Maverick should have the edge on any of them," said Grandpa.

"Finally, some real power!" said Maverick. "I don't know about you, Jimmy, but I'm hungry for first place. Let's test them out!"

"Okey dokey!" said Grandpa. "Stand back!"

Jimmy ducked and covered his eyebrows as he ran out of the way. Grandpa leaned into Maverick's cockpit and checked that the handbrake was on. Then he flicked a switch on Maverick's dashboard and the flame shot out, making the robot lurch forward. If the handbrake hadn't been on, Maverick would have taken off like a firework!

"Not bad, eh?" said Grandpa as he calmly reached for a fire extinguisher and sprayed it at a nearby workbench that had caught fire. Jimmy had a suspicion it wasn't the first time he'd had to use it today.

"Needs a little adjustment, but it's almost there. During the race, you'll only be able to use the blasters for a short period," he added. "We need to be careful with the nitro-blasters, though. They're very delicate. If they're not treated right, they could be dangerous."

"How dangerous?" Jimmy asked.

Grandpa didn't answer, but Jimmy saw him glance guiltily up at the ceiling, where a large black burn mark was still smoking. He hurried to the other side of the lab.

Jimmy noticed how busy the workshop looked. Experiments were taking place everywhere. Chemicals were bubbling on burners, machines were opening and shutting parachutes, spinning tires smoked, and lights were blinking off and on.

A strange contraption in the corner was pouring hot brown liquid into a glass beaker. Grandpa took it, peered into it, shook it around for a bit, and sipped at the contents.

"Automatic tea maker," he said. "Most important machine in this shed."

"Except for Maverick," Jimmy said with a laugh. "Will we be ready for the next race?"

"The Rain Forest Rampage? Of course we will!" said Maverick. "I'm like a new robot! I'm tuned up and ready to go! My engine is in better shape, I've had a full buff and polish, and all my bulbs have been changed. Hey, Grandpa! Let's show Jimmy some of my latest modifications."

Grandpa had just sat down in his favorite chair in the corner of the lab. "Can't a man grab a quick cup of tea in peace?" he grumbled. He got back to his feet, passed Jimmy his tea, and climbed into Maverick's passenger seat.

"Why does this smell like gas?" asked Jimmy, sniffing the thick brown tea.

"It's just how I like it," shrugged Grandpa. "Now, the next race is in the jungles of South America, so I thought we should be prepared for whatever Lord Loonpipe has up his fancy sleeves."

"Leadpipe," corrected Jimmy. He knew that Grandpa hated Lord Leadpipe, but he had good reason. The billionaire had made his fortune from ideas he'd stolen from Grandpa's lab. And Jimmy knew that was why Grandpa wanted Jimmy to win the Robot Races Championship so badly.

Grandpa carried on. "The jungle is very swampy. In case we run into some quicksand, I've installed an EFD."

"What's an EFD?" Jimmy replied.

"Glad you asked!" Grandpa grinned. "It's an Emergency Floatation Device." He reached across the dashboard and hit a button. Jimmy heard a loud hissing sound. From underneath Maverick a sheet of orange rubber appeared and rapidly started to fill with air. Maverick soon had an inflatable cushion around him, like he was wearing a bright orange skirt.

"It suits you, Maverick!" Jimmy laughed.

"You don't think it looks like I'm wearing a dress?" asked Maverick anxiously.

Jimmy tried to hide a grin. "No, I think you look very stylish."

Grandpa hit another button and a compartment in the hood opened up. "If we get into a tight spot," he said, "I've installed some grappling hooks. Just press this button and they'll shoot out and pull you to safety."

He pushed the button. Two pronged hooks made out of bits of scrap metal and wire flew out from Maverick's hood. The sharp hooks bounced off the ceiling, whistled past Jimmy's right ear, and plunged straight into Maverick's inflatable EFD.

A loud hiss filled the room.

"I guess I'll fetch the puncture repair kit," said Grandpa with a sheepish grin, getting out of Maverick and hurrying across the workshop.

"Come and have a seat, Jimmy," said Maverick, his other door popping open. "There's a nice surprise inside."

Jimmy went around to the driver's seat and sat down. He saw that Grandpa had updated the dashboard. Where the old radio used to be, there were now more confusing gadgets and switches and buttons than ever, including a TV.

"Awesome!" yelled Jimmy, settling into the comfy seat. "What's on, Maverick?"

"Just one channel, Jimmy," said Maverick.

"The Robo TV channel!" they said together.

Robo TV was a channel that only showed Robot Races. It had all the big competitions and got all the best interviews with racers and their robots. Jimmy switched it on and waited for it to warm up.

Everything that Grandpa installed into Maverick was reused and recycled, including the TV. Grandpa had used his electronic wizardry to turn it into a multi-functional touch-screen TV with optional voice commands. It needed a firm whack with the palm of Jimmy's hand to get going, but it was still pretty impressive.

The picture finally cleared. Jimmy recognized the face of Brent Hasburger, Robo TV's smooth anchorman. Brent sat behind a desk and introduced the warm-up to the next race.

"I hope you brought your sunscreen, race fans, because the competition is hot, hot, hot! We're coming to you live from Manaus, Brazil, where preparations are underway for the second race of this special Robot Races championship."

"This is so cool!" said Jimmy. "Maybe we'll get some new information on the track."

Brent Hasburger smoothed down his oily black hair and smiled at the camera. "Of course, we don't have any more information about the track —"

"Oh," Jimmy sighed.

"— as those details are being kept top secret. Jenny Velour is at the site. What do you know, Jenny?"

The image changed to show a reporter with a microphone. Behind her was a giant steel wall with some trees poking over the top.

"Thank you, Brent. Lord Leadpipe's track builders have been in this area of the Amazon for weeks now, designing and building the new race track. Secrecy is very important. The area has been fenced off so people are not able to see inside. Aircraft have even been banned from flying overhead, in case someone takes a photograph of the site from the air. We know little about the layout ... well, we don't know anything at all actually. Not even the racers know what will happen to them in this epic two-day race, but the experts have come up with a few suspected features."

"They're not being much help, are they?" Jimmy sighed. "They're just guessing!"

The screen now showed images of the jungle and the dangers that Jimmy might come across.

"Lord Leadpipe has been known to leave the track as a mud road for some of the previous competitions. The humid weather will make for a very soggy track, so off-road tires might be a smart move. Quicksand is also a danger —"

"Told you!" said Grandpa, who had just stepped back into the shed.

"— so is the risk of mud slides on the higher land and trees falling across the track. The jungle will also be full of wild animals. Our brave racers will have to be on their guard during their overnight stop, just in case one of these fearsome fellows decides to visit."

The screen showed jaguars, spiders, and insects looking menacing. Jimmy started to feel nervous.

"Don't worry, Jimmy!" said Maverick. "If we can cope with Horace Pelly and that robot of his, we can cope with a few creepy-crawly spiders!"

"No one knows what challenges Lord Leadpipe himself has planned," continued Jenny. "But we suspect that the contestants will stay overnight at this luxury campsite in the very heart of the jungle."

"Ooooh . . ." said Jimmy as the TV showed aerial pictures of a beautiful jungle clearing, with ladders leading up tall trees. Small huts had been built into the tree canopies, with rope bridges linking them. There was even a building that looked like a deluxe garage facility for all the robots to sleep in.

"That looks very fancy!" said Grandpa. "I hope they've got tea-making machines."

Brent Hasburger reappeared on the screen. "And now let's hear what the contenders have to say about the upcoming challenge."

First came Missy, the loud Australian with the monster truck. She was tinkering with

Monster's oil while talking loudly to the camera: "You think I'm afraid of a few jungle creepy crawlies? In Australia, we have spiders that can bite your arm off! As for the track, there isn't one built that I couldn't drive Monster through blindfolded."

The interviewer laughed politely.

"No, really!" said Missy. "We've been practicing. It's a little hit and miss at the moment." The camera scanned over Missy's backyard, showing a number of crushed cars.

Next was Kako, the Japanese princess. She sat and played a game on her 3D phone while the interviewer tried to get her attention. In the background sat Lightning, her super robobike, with five technicians polishing him and topping off his brake fluid.

"I'm sure the course will be very exciting." She yawned, not even raising her eyes to the camera. "I'm looking forward to the challenge. I've worked very hard to make Lightning the best of the best." She pointed over her shoulder, where Lightning revved his loud engine.

"They should come and interview you, Jimmy!" said Grandpa. "You'd give 'em a good show, eh?" He took off his hat and scratched his head, sending his untidy white hair into several different directions. "Come to think of it, why haven't you been interviewed yet?"

Jimmy shrugged and turned his attention back to the tiny TV.

Chip, the American contestant, sat in his yellow digger-like robot, Dug. "I just want a fair race," he said with a thick Southern accent. "I got tricked last time when Horace and Zoom decided to play dirty. Well, that ain't gonna happen again, let me tell you. I'll be watching you, Horace, and you'll be watching my taillights as I speed into first place!"

"He's a little competitive!" said Grandpa.

"Chip? He's okay," Jimmy replied, thinking about how he'd helped the Southern boy in the last race. Chip disliked Horace almost as much as he did!

The TV screen changed again to show a dry, sandy landscape. The hot sun beat down on the desert. A giant air-cushioned hovercraft came speeding across the sand with an enormous roar.

The robot racer Maximus came to a stop in a cloud of dust. The central cab opened and Samir, a quiet Egyptian boy in a simple T-shirt and jeans, got out. He was followed by his father, Omar, who was always by his side. The interviewer offered the microphone to Sammy, but it was immediately snatched by his father.

"Thank you, thank you! Samir is pleased you have come to support him. Soon we travel to South America, where we will crush the opposition! I remember when I raced in Peru almost twenty years ago . . ."

Sammy's father continued on with a tale of his own time in the Robot Races Championships, while Sammy stood next to him looking uncomfortable. Every time a question was asked, Omar would jump in and interrupt.

Thud! Thud! Thud!

Jimmy and Grandpa stood and stared at the door. No one had ever knocked at the door of the secret shed before. Even Jimmy hadn't known it existed until a few weeks ago. Grandpa approached the door carefully.

Thud! Thud! Thud!

The two stared at each other, not sure what to do.

"Come on, get a move on!" said Maverick. "It might be one of my fans asking for an autograph!"

Grandpa squeezed the door open, then closed it again and turned to Jimmy.

"You know I said someone should interview you? Well, I think they've arrived!"

He let the door swing open to reveal a deafening crowd of journalists with cameras and microphones, all shouting for Jimmy!

CHAPTER 3
FAME AT LAST

"Jimmy! Jimmy!"

"Jimmy Roberts, over here!"

"What's it like to be the underdog?"

"What do you think about the other contestants?"

Everyone was shouting all at once, pushing microphones at Jimmy. Flashbulbs were going off like crazy. Jimmy stood in the doorway to the shed, stunned at the group of journalists who had suddenly appeared in his backyard.

"I . . . er . . . um . . ." he floundered, his mouth opening and closing. He really couldn't believe this was happening.

"Go on, Jimmy, they're waiting for you," said Grandpa with an encouraging nudge.

Maverick trundled up the ramp behind them. "I knew they'd finally find me! Give my hood a quick polish, please. I want to look my best for the photos," he said excitedly.

The sound in the yard rose, and Jimmy felt overwhelmed by the attention. No one had ever wanted to interview him before, and certainly not fifty people at once. He stepped back and started to close the door.

"I'm sorry, I —"

Just then he caught sight of a woman in the front row, dressed in a blue dress. She had silvery hair, which was tied up in a bun. She was waiting quietly and patiently, her microphone clutched to her chest. She smiled warmly at Jimmy as he looked at her.

Jimmy recognized her at once. It was Bet Bristle, Robo TV's oldest broadcaster. Jimmy had been watching her all his life! She had interviewed all the great racers over the years and now she was looking at him.

"Y-you're Bet Bristle!" he stammered. The crowd went quiet.

"That's right, dear. I was wondering if I might ask you a few questions for Robo TV?" she said politely. Over her shoulder, Jimmy could see the other journalists jostling each other to try and hear their conversation. He couldn't believe this was happening!

"Me? Yes, of course."

"Excellent. Let's get you with Maverick, shall we?" she said, her eyes darting to Grandpa, who broke out in a blush. Even though he hated Lord Leadpipe, he had always liked Bet.

Grandpa pressed a few buttons and the whole front of the garden shed rose up like a garage door. Maverick drove up the ramp and out to meet the crowd. He bounced his hood playfully and flashed his lights at the photographers like he'd been used to fame for years.

"This is the life!" said Maverick.

Grandpa rolled his eyes. Jimmy leaned on Maverick's hood, trying to look casual as Bet started her interview.

"How are you enjoying being a robot racer?" she said with a smile, holding out her microphone.

"I love it!" Jimmy blurted out. The crowd laughed, and he felt encouraged to go on. "It's been great to compete against the other robots. It's all been kind of a whirlwind, but I've enjoyed every second. Also, it means I get to spend lots of time with my grandpa. He's the chief technician. Actually, he's our only technician."

The crowd laughed again.

"So do you think you can win?" said Bet.

"You bet we can!" shouted Maverick.

Jimmy silenced him with a gentle pat on the bumper. "I don't know," he said humbly. "There are so many great racers. We were lucky to take second place last time. I just hope we can do it again."

Bet smiled and glanced at the crowd of reporters.

"I think he's being modest!" she said in a stage whisper. This was greeted with a chuckle and some nodding heads in the crowd. "And what have you got in store for your next race, Jimmy? It looks as though Maverick has had a bit of a makeover."

Jimmy guided Bet over to Maverick, showing her the new TV and the array of buttons on the dashboard.

"Grandpa's just added some new nitro-blasters, which should speed us up too," he said proudly. "And the jungle can be full of dangers, so we're fully equipped with lots of gadgets to get us out of tight spots."

"How clever," said Bet, flashing a smile at Grandpa. He smiled back and went a deep shade of pink.

Jimmy was getting really excited. The crowd was keen to hear what he had to say, and he felt more confident by the second.

"We're ready for anything! Bring it on, Amazon! We've planned for mud slides, quicksand, wild animals, snakes —"

"Snakes?" Maverick said, and Jimmy darted out of the way as Maverick started to shake.

Bet looked confused as Maverick's wheels whirred and spun on the spot, as if he was trying to speed away.

"Maverick! Stop!" Grandpa jumped into the driver's seat and pulled on the robot's handbrake again.

"You never mentioned snakes!" mumbled Maverick, his electronic voice shaking. He gave a blast of his new nitro-blasters, which sent the crowd diving to the ground. His body shook again, and a puff of smoke rose up from the dashboard. Maverick lay still for a moment, and Grandpa climbed back out again.

"He's overheated! He'll be all right when he calms down," he said. "Sounds like the old thing is afraid of snakes!"

Bet turned to face her TV camera and spoke into her microphone. "There you have it. Jimmy Roberts, the fearless underdog of the Robot Races championship, and Maverick, his not-so-fearless companion. This is Bet Bristle for Robo TV."

CHAPTER 4
A MESSAGE

The crowd of reporters piled into their cars. Every one of them was shouting into a phone about the weird press conference.

"That's right," one said. "A panic attack. The robot had a panic attack!"

"He's scared of snakes! Can you believe that?" said another.

Jimmy and Grandpa pushed Maverick back into the shed. When Maverick finally came back online, he sounded shy and bashful.

"Maverick, why are you afraid of snakes?" asked Jimmy.

"I don't like how they move. Slippery little things," the robot racer said. Jimmy was sure he felt the robot shudder.

"But you're a robot. How can a robot be afraid of anything?"

"It's my built-in personality technology. I'm programmed to be chirpy and happy and ophidiophobic." Grandpa and Jimmy stared at the robot blankly. "It means I'm afraid of snakes," Maverick explained. "Keep up."

"Well, can we reprogram you?" Jimmy asked.

"Change my personality?" Maverick said in shock. "I'm not a toaster, you know."

"He's right," Grandpa chipped in. "If we start messing around with his circuits, he could lose his current personality altogether. And we don't want to do that, do we?"

"No, definitely not," said Jimmy. "I wouldn't change you for the world."

"Well, okay then," Maverick said, a little calmer. "Just keep me away from any snakes and we'll be fine, Jimmy."

Just then there was another knock at the door. Grandpa got up and went to open it. "Sorry, no more interviews today!" he said as he opened the door. He stopped as soon as he saw that the person outside was not a journalist, but a short man in thick glasses and a lab coat. Jimmy noticed the familiar L on his jacket. He was from Leadpipe Industries.

"Who are you?" said Grandpa.

"I'm afraid that is classified information," said the man in a thin, whiny voice. He barged past Grandpa into the shed. "I'm here on official Robot Races business. Is this your robot?" he asked, pointing at Maverick.

"No, it's the washing machine," snapped Grandpa, "Of course he's our robot."

The man reached into his pocket and brought out a small computer chip held in a pair of tweezers.

"I've been ordered to make an essential upgrade, by order of Lord Leadpipe himself. Excuse me." He reached past Jimmy and clipped the computer chip to the dashboard.

"Now hang on!" said Grandpa. "No one fiddles with Maverick except me!"

"I think you'll find the upgrade will come in useful," he said, pushing his glasses up his nose. "You may need to reboot the system for it to take effect. Nice work on the circuit board. Did you use special wire?"

"Er, no. Lead-free," said Grandpa, sounding confused.

The man nodded, impressed. "Good choice," he said, and left without another word.

"What a strange chap," said Grandpa. "Go on then, let's see what Loonpipe has given us."

After a few minutes of fiddling, the TV came back on. On it was the familiar spinning Leadpipe Industries logo and small icon reading "Welcome."

"Grandpa, what's this?" asked Jimmy.

"Beats me," said Grandpa. Jimmy touched the welcome icon. The screen filled with the face of Lord Leadpipe.

"What does he want?" asked Grandpa in a crabby voice.

"Greetings, Racer!" said Lord Leadpipe. "Thank you for accepting the RoboNet upgrade. It is the secure private network made exclusively for robot racers."

"I didn't accept it!" said Grandpa.

"Your TV has been updated to become Cabcom, a multi-feature communications station. You can use it to talk to the other racers in the competition and with your technical team in the pit stop during races. Enjoy!"

The screen went blue, but a small envelope popped onto the screen.

"We've got a message!" said Jimmy excitedly. He tapped his finger over the envelope and some more details appeared:

TO: MAVERICK
FROM: ZOOM

"Oh, no," Jimmy said with a sigh. He thought about whether to open the message. Then he pressed it — although as he did it, he wasn't sure if it was a good idea.

It wasn't.

Horace Pelly's smug face filled the screen. It was a recorded video message.

"Jimmy, hi! I thought I'd leave you a quick message to wish you good luck for the race. After all, you're going to need it in that rust bucket."

Jimmy stuck his tongue out at the screen.

"My NASA guys have been improving Zoom," Horace continued. "He is totally ready for the jungle." Behind him, the screen showed a number of people working on Zoom. "They've just finished my new laser guidance system, which is the most advanced guidance technology in the world. They invented it especially for me."

He produced a handheld PC, which glowed with pretty lights and maps on the screen. "A satellite of my very own that tracks where I am at all times. Just look at this thing! It's incredible."

On the screen, Horace started laughing. "Good press conference, by the way. Very informative. Later, losers! I've got a race to win. See you in the jungle!" He laughed, then disappeared off the screen.

Jimmy was worried now. He followed Grandpa into the house and had some juice and sandwiches.

"Don't worry about Horace Smelly. He's just a bully," said Grandpa as he handed Jimmy a letter to read.

Dear Mr. Roberts,

Congratulations on your recent success in the Robot Races Championship. Myself and my company would like to offer some financial support in the way of a sponsorship.

"Yes! Our first sponsorship deal!" said Jimmy, punching the air.

"It gets better. Keep reading," said Grandpa.

That's Shallot! is Smedingham's leading supplier of fruit and vegetables. We are willing to extend a generous offer in return for advertising on the side of your wonderful robot, Maverick.

"Hang on. It's a fruit and vegetable supplier? I thought it might be someone cool," Jimmy said with a frown.

"They're as cool as a cucumber, Jimmy! Get it?" Grandpa laughed. "All right, it might not be Speed-ease Trainers, but they're offering quite a deal."

Jimmy read on.

If you agree, we will provide a special, top-of-the-line Carrot Vision Night Visor, as well as some more home comforts for your upcoming races. We know you might not have mushroom in your schedule, but lettuce make you a sponsorship offer you can't turnip your nose at. We hope someone hasn't beet us to it!

Have a good thyme at the race!

Sincerely,

Felix Crump

Jimmy groaned at the awful puns. He was embarrassed at the thought of advertising a fruit and vegetable company. Other robots had Luke's Lasers or Robotron Rocket Boots plastered

down their sides. Then he thought back to
Horace's video message and the huge team
of NASA experts buzzing around Zoom. He'd
never be able to afford that sort of support.

Jimmy sighed. *I guess a bad sponsor is better
than no sponsor,* he thought. *And I don't want
Grandpa to think I'm ungrateful.*

"That's great news, Grandpa," he said aloud,
forcing a broad smile onto his face.

"Excellent! We'll call to accept their offer in
the morning," said the old man. He got up and
drank the rest of his hot tea, patting Jimmy on
the shoulder as he walked out of the room.

Jimmy smiled, but deep down he was
worried about the race ahead. *I've got a feeling
I'm going to need all the help I can get,* he thought.

★ ★ ★

Jimmy and Grandpa sat in the fancy
restaurant in Lord Leadpipe's airship as it
floated away from Smedingham. They were
being treated to a first-class menu from

Leadpipe's personal chef. But despite the relaxing surroundings, soothing music, and amazing food, Jimmy had never felt so nervous. Big Al had said he was the one to beat, but he wondered if he could actually live up to the hype.

Before leaving he had watched Robo TV for hours, finding out what he could about the upgrades the other racers had put on their robots. Chip had chosen special mud-grip tires. Princess Kako had added Computer Assisted Stabilizing Technology (CAST) so that her bike wouldn't fall over, especially when caught in the wet mud of the jungle. His Carrot Vision Visor didn't seem like much of an upgrade at all.

He wanted to talk to Maverick, but he was at the back of the airship with the other robots. He'd know what to say. He'd be his usual upbeat and cheery self. He would tell Jimmy how they were going to win fair and square, using just their wits and smarts to get to first place.

Instead Jimmy hunched lower in his plush leather chair and picked at his meal as the aircraft accelerated to hyper speed without the slightest vibration.

"Ladies and gentlemen, we are now approaching your destination. Please put on your seat belts as we prepare to land."

Jimmy looked around. It had only been a couple of hours, but the super-fast airship had transported them all the way to South America. Grandpa put down his Robot Owner's Technical Manual and smiled. "Time to get this show on the road, Jimmy!"

Outside the window, Jimmy could see a blanket of green across the land. Through the jungle ran a wide river, snaking its way through the landscape. As they descended, Jimmy could just begin to make out a shape under the trees. It was the Robot Races track, winding in and out of the rain forest. He also saw a small clearing, which he assumed would be their base camp.

"Ready to race, Jimmy?" asked Grandpa.

Jimmy smiled nervously. "Ready as I'll ever be!"

CHAPTER 5
BASE CAMP

Jimmy and Grandpa slowly walked down the long walkway from the airship. They found themselves in a jungle clearing. They walked out onto the ground, their feet sinking into the soft mud.

The first thing to hit Jimmy, apart from the heat and dampness, was how far away they were from anybody. He had assumed they would land to a large, cheering crowd. It looked like Lord Leadpipe had other plans.

"I guess they don't want anyone to see us," said a voice from behind them. It was Chip, in his usual baseball cap and jeans. "That's got to be the only reason to throw us this far out into the jungle!"

"I think you're right," said Jimmy. "And it's so hot and sticky out here."

"Yeah," Chip drawled. "I think I'll take a shower in my trailer."

"Trailer?" said Grandpa.

"Didn't y'all know our sponsors have been asked to provide our accommodations?" said Chip. "Here's mine now. See ya on the track!"

"Accommodations? I can't see any accommodations," said Grandpa.

"Look over there," said Jimmy.

From the airship, an enormous robotic arm lowered a huge silver trailer into position in the clearing. The words "Chip & Dug — Sponsored by Luke's Lasers" were on the side. Chip disappeared through the door. A moment later, Jimmy could make out the sound of rock music coming from inside.

Jimmy and Grandpa watched the robotic arm place the other trailers in the clearing. Missy's was a large rough-and-ready trailer with the name of her sponsor, Robotron Rocket Boots, down one side. She hopped inside, where Jimmy could see a plush sofa and game station with huge speakers.

Princess Kako's trailer was an elegant white cube. At first it looked small and modest, but when Kako pressed a button, each side expanded upward and outward until it became a three-story palace. Servants came out to greet her, each offering a tray of refreshments.

"Don't worry, Jimmy. I'm sure That's Shallot! has figured out something for us," said Grandpa with a nervous smile.

"Um, I think this may be ours," said Jimmy, pointing to the robotic arm coming down. As it slowly came down, they could see the bottom of the trailer spotted with rust. Jimmy gave a sigh. It was an old beige trailer with flat tires and cracked windows.

On the side, in letters that were already peeling off, were the words "That's Shallot!" Jimmy groaned with embarrassment. Grandpa ripped off a note stuck to the door:

Dear Mr. Roberts,

Please accept this as a token of support. While you're preparing for victory in the jungle, we at That's Shallot! thought you might need some comfort and food. This trailer has air conditioning, cooling technology, and is filled with reminders of home. It may be a bit of a squash, but chive got a feeling you'll love it!

Good luck, old bean!

Felix Crump

Grandpa and Jimmy squeezed through the narrow door. Inside, it was so hot you could bake a potato.

"Where's the air conditioning?" said Grandpa.

Jimmy held up a tiny desk fan that sat on the table.

"And the cooling technology?"

"I think they mean the fridge," said Jimmy.

He opened it to find it packed with broccoli. The door of the fridge contained rows of cans of energizing juice. Each can read "Made from the finest ingredients, including over twelve servings of vegetables per can!" Jimmy slammed the door of the fridge closed and stepped back outside.

"Hey, Jimmy! Nice digs!" shouted a familiar voice. Jimmy and Grandpa turned to see Horace with his toothy grin, standing next to his own trailer. "I could only afford a secondhand trailer too."

The trailer in question was white with some black markings on it. Jimmy had the feeling that he'd seen it somewhere before.

"Is that a space shuttle?" he said.

"This old thing?" Horace looked up. "The NASA boys had an old one lying around, so Dad got them to turn it into a trailer for me. It just has the basics — flat-screen TV, 3D gaming system, king-sized bed. You know, the usual."

"Ignore him, Jimmy," said Grandpa. "It doesn't matter who's got the fanciest trailer. It's all about winning the race."

"Oh, I'm going to win that as well!" said Horace. "I have the best trailer and the best robot. It would be impossible for me to lose. Look, here he comes now."

The robotic arm lowered Zoom into place beside the shuttle. Zoom's lights flashed as he said hello to Horace.

"Good trip, Zoom?" said Horace.

"Yes, thank you, Horace."

"Good. Zoom, show the nice people your new guidance system."

Zoom obediently powered up, and Jimmy watched as a grid of red lasers shone from the nose of the engine.

"The multi-point laser guidance system measures the local terrain to produce a special map," said Zoom, sounding like a shop demonstration model. "This is fed to the auto steering system, which will allow for differences in track height and width."

Horace smiled. Jimmy noticed the whole camp was watching. Sammy, the quiet Egyptian boy, had appeared by his side. Although Sammy didn't talk much, Jimmy liked him. He was nice and an excellent racer.

"Dad says it's the best," Horace continued. "He's spoken to Lord Leadpipe personally."

Jimmy ignored him and turned to see Maverick being lowered from the big airship. Grandpa went to make sure Maverick was okay after his trip.

"Zoom, scan the area for snakes. We don't want poor Maverick to be scared, do we?" said Horace.

A grid of lasers scanned the clearing. "No reptiles detected."

"Really?" said Horace with a grin. "We'll see about that." He disappeared into his trailer, laughing the whole way.

"Am I understanding this?" Sammy asked. "The Zoom robot will measure the distances between the trees and swamps, meaning that Horace does not even have to steer?"

"Yup," said Jimmy.

"But this is an outrage!" said Sammy. "And surely against the rules of robot racing? Why have a race with someone who does not drive? I can't believe this!"

Jimmy was glad someone else had noticed Horace's cheating. "Horace has never really paid any attention to rules," he said. "I think that NASA put that guidance system in so that they could avoid the one faulty part in the team — Horace."

They both laughed. Jimmy was just about to see if Sammy wanted a vegetable juice drink when they heard a shout from Sammy's trailer.

"Samir! Come here now! There is much work to be done!" Omar stuck his head out of their trailer and scowled at the boys.

"Father, I was just speaking to Jimmy —"

"No time for that! Come now. We will have race tactics training!"

Sammy shrugged to Jimmy, then headed slowly back to his trailer. Jimmy wandered over to Maverick and Grandpa. His grandpa was now sipping a can of veggie juice drink.

"What's it like?" asked Jimmy.

"Kind of like my world-famous cabbage stew," Grandpa said, smacking his lips together. "I am hungry just thinking about it."

"Yuck!" said Jimmy, thinking how much his grandpa's cabbage stew actually tasted like old socks.

"Come on, let's get Maverick tuned up," Grandpa said.

The clearing was soon filled with the roar of engines as each team made their final adjustments.

"How are you feeling, Maverick?" asked Jimmy.

"I could do with a top-up of coolant. It's hot out here!"

"Me too," said Grandpa. "I'll put the kettle on."

Jimmy laughed. "Grandpa, how can you drink a hot cup of tea in this heat?"

"I'm made of strong stuff!" he joked. "And so is the tea." He went inside the trailer.

"If it isn't our underdog!" Lord Leadpipe's voice boomed. The billionaire was walking around the clearing, strolling proudly around the area, shaking hands with contestants and their families.

"I must say, your robot is spectacular! The others are very slick, but Maverick has a certain charm."

"Are you trying to say my robot is amateurish, Leadpipe?" Grandpa stood in the doorway of the trailer, a steaming cup of tea in his hand. He glared at Leadpipe, his eyes squinting.

"Wilfred," said Leadpipe, surprised. "I didn't see you there for a moment. Quite the robot, as I was saying. Have you —"

"Increased the coolant levels? Yes."

"Oh. And did you —"

"Add anti-quicksand technology? Of course."

"Right. I suppose you —"

"Adjusted tire pressure for the soft mud track. Yes, Ludwick, I did."

An uneasy silence spread through the jungle. Even the monkeys and the parrots in the trees seemed to stop their screeching in order to watch the two old men stare each other out.

"Yes, well. Some wise upgrades. Good luck to you." Lord Leadpipe started to stroll off.

"Yes, I do know a thing or two about robots," mumbled Grandpa. "As some people know, I've been inventing them for years."

Lord Leadpipe stopped dead in his tracks, and turned slowly back to face Grandpa, who folded his arms and looked pointedly back. The billionaire seemed genuinely confused, his smooth, confident manner shaken for a moment.

AWOOGA! AWOOGA!

They were interrupted by a siren echoing through the forest, followed by an electronic voice.

"FIVE MINUTES TO RACE TIME. REPEAT: FIVE MINUTES TO RACE TIME."

Lord Leadpipe consulted his pocket watch and marched off, his assistants following behind.

"Okay, if everyone's finished with the small talk," said Maverick, revving his engine excitedly, "we've got a race to win!"

CHAPTER 6
GO!

Maverick screeched to a halt on the start
line. Since they had finished in second place in
the last race, they lined up right behind Princess
Kako and Lightning.

"Are you ready, Jimmy?" Maverick asked.

"I think so," said Jimmy. "Just nervous. You?"

"Nervous? Me? No way! This is what I was
built for. Can't wait!"

The TV on Maverick's dashboard fizzed and
crackled. Jimmy hit it a few times with his palm
until the image became clear. It was Grandpa.
He was wearing a large pair of headphones
over his wild white hair. He had a funny little

microphone next to his mouth and was yelling very loudly into it.

"BASE TO MAVERICK! BASE TO MAVERICK! ARE YOU RECEIVING? OVER."

Jimmy had to cover his ears. "Grandpa, there's no need to shout! Yes, we can hear you."

"Sorry!" said Grandpa with a grin. "I'm used to my old taxi radio. Anyway, I'll keep in touch and contact you when you need to come into the pit stop. Just remember to keep your wits about you. I'm cheering for you, kid! Good luck!"

Jimmy took a deep breath and looked around. There was Princess Kako and Lightning in front of him. Chip and his racer Dug were directly behind him. Horace was behind Chip, shouting orders to the NASA crew who were performing last-minute checks on Zoom. Next was Monster, the huge four-wheeled beast driven by Missy. She revved the engine so loudly that Monster sounded like a jumbo jet.

At the very back was the huge hovercraft-like robot, Maximus, piloted by Sammy. His father was shouting from the sidelines. To Jimmy it sounded more like he was bossing his son around rather than encouraging him. "Remember, Samir, full throttle!" he yelled. "Take no prisoners! Failure is not an option!"

Wow, thought Jimmy. *Samir's dad was really serious about this race.*

The Leadpipe Industries airship and lots of cameras were flying above the racers. They were streaming the race live to fans across the world. Thousands of fans who had been allowed into the enormous grandstands lined the track. They were yelling and clapping like crazy! Some fans held up signs and banners.

Jimmy noticed that a few signs even had his name on them, which made him feel good. One said, "COME ON, MAVERICK!" Another read, "WE LOVE JIMMY!"

"Looks like we're starting! Better put on a show for our fans, eh, Jimmy?" said Maverick as Jimmy pulled his battered old helmet on. The front of it was painted with the That's Shallot! onion logo to match the one that had been painted on Maverick. It wasn't fancy, but it would keep him safe.

The crowd hushed as the engines revved. Lord Leadpipe stood at the start line, a microphone in his hand.

"Five!" he yelled, his voice echoing over the loudspeakers.

"Four!" This time the crowd joined in.

"Three! Two!"

The last second seemed to last for a lifetime.

"One! Go, go, GO!" Leadpipe shouted.

The race was on!

Tires squealed, wheels spun, and everything was a blur. The robots struggled to get a grip on the road, and then they suddenly lurched forward. Jimmy was thrown back in his seat as Maverick accelerated at a tremendous pace. He tapped the gear paddle once, twice, three times as Maverick picked up speed.

Alongside him Princess Kako and Lightning were making a good start, easing away from the competition and positioning themselves for the best angle into the first corner.

Jimmy felt the ground rumbling dangerously. He checked his rearview mirror to see Chip and Dug behind him, powering forward until they were right on Maverick's tail. The size of the digger-like robot was terrifying. The deep noise from the large engine drowned out the high-pitched revs coming from underneath Maverick's hood. Chip was having no trouble steering Dug's track wheels on the clay roads, but Maverick's tires were slipping and sliding.

"Take it a little bit slower," said Maverick. "We don't want to risk a crash."

Jimmy eased off the gas slightly and took the turn cautiously, allowing Chip room to pull alongside. Behind them, Monster's giant wheels were also tearing up the terrain. Missy dived to the right of Jimmy, and for a moment he was boxed between two giant robot racers.

The noise of their engines was deafening. The ground was shaking so much they could easily have been in the middle of an earthquake. There was so much shaking Jimmy could barely hold the steering wheel. He was almost relieved when the two heavy vehicles sped past him. But it did mean that Jimmy and Maverick moved into fourth place.

"See ya!" shouted Missy as she cruised past the rest of them and into the lead. As Monster increased in speed, the giant tires kicked up mud and sprayed it all over the other robots.

"Yuck!" said Jimmy. "Maverick, I'm turning on the wipers."

Maverick and Maximus were neck and neck now. Jimmy glanced across to see Sammy blinded by the mud splattered over his windshield. He was panicking in his cab.

Jimmy flicked on the Cabcom screen and pressed on a button that said SAMIR AND MAXIMUS. The Cabcom immediately showed Sammy in the driver's seat, desperately searching for a button. "You okay, Sammy?" Jimmy asked.

"Yes. Aha, got it!" Sammy said, flicking a switch. "Oops —" he added as a burst of fire lifted Maximus high into the air. He bunny-hopped down the track and spun in a full circle before coming to a stop.

"Look out!" Maverick yelled. Jimmy had been so busy watching Sammy he'd forgotten to pay attention to his own driving. He had to swerve wildly to avoid a curtain of vines hanging down. He veered to the other side of the track. He managed to skid past them without slowing down, but Zoom wasn't so lucky. Horace must have seen the vines too late. Horace hit them full on, sending Zoom spinning out of control.

"Yikes!" said Jimmy with a smile. "That'll slow them down for a bit."

It took all of his concentration to keep Maverick on the road for the next twenty miles. The track was proving to be a bigger challenge than his fellow racers. It had huge holes in the road and hidden tree stumps and vines to avoid. Jimmy was glad he could rely on Maverick's navigation to help him avoid an accident.

"We haven't seen any of the others for ages," Jimmy said after a while. "I'm beginning to think we'll never catch Dug, Monster, or Lightning."

But just then they passed a flash of silver on the roadside. Princess Kako was covered in mud.

As Maverick whizzed on by, Jimmy could see a furious Kako using all her strength to pull a sharp stake of wood from Lightning's back tire. She had a serious puncture.

"She won't like that," said Jimmy. "I wonder if she'll be able to fix it."

"She'll be fine," replied Maverick. "Once she gets that chunk of tree out of Lightning he'll activate his automatic tire repair system. They'll be back on our tail in no time if we don't hurry, so let's get moving!"

"Good point. Let's do this!" yelled Jimmy.

Over the next few miles the road got smoother. They slowly began to close the gap on the racers in front. Soon Jimmy could see Dug in the distance, thundering along the course.

"It's time to unleash our special weapon," said Maverick. "The track widens up ahead. It might be a good opportunity to overtake on Chip's right."

"What? We'll never be able to get past before the road narrows again!" Jimmy exclaimed. "It's too risky!"

"Calm down. That's where these come in," said Maverick, and a small button lit up on the dashboard, flashing blue.

Jimmy recognized it. The nitro-blasters. He gulped.

"Come on, Jimmy. You worry too much!" said Maverick.

"All right," Jimmy answered, bracing himself. "Let's see what you can do."

"Yes! Hold onto your helmet, Jimmy!" the robot replied.

Jimmy positioned Maverick to the right of the track and reached out to the flashing blue button. He held on tight and pressed it.

The next thing Jimmy knew, his head was pressed against his racing seat like it was superglued to it. Maverick was flying along the track faster than a fighter jet!

CHAPTER 7
SONIC BOOM

"Woo-hoo!" shouted Maverick as they were propelled forward by the nitro-blaster.

"Aaaaaaagh!" screamed Jimmy, his hands gripping the steering wheel so tightly that he left marks where his fingernails had dug in.

Maverick zoomed ahead, a ribbon of blue flame licking out of the boosters mounted on each side of him. The camerabots had to spin around overhead to keep up with them, and they were still accelerating.

"This . . . is . . . amazing!" Jimmy yelled.

"We've still got the best part to come — the sonic boom!" said Maverick, who was clearly loving every second. He was so excited Jimmy thought Maverick might burst!

"Sonic what?" Jimmy gasped out.

"Never mind. Brace yourself. Three . . . Two . . . One . . ."

BOOM!

Beautiful birds of paradise scattered and monkeys screeched behind them as they raced through the forest.

They drew alongside Dug. But they were running out of space. The track was getting narrower and narrower, and they were approaching a sharp left turn.

"We're not going to make it!" yelled Maverick. "There's no way we can turn the corner at this speed!"

"We'll make it!" said Jimmy over the loud engine. "Do you trust me?"

"What? Why?"

"I've got a plan. Do you trust me?"

"Yes!"

"Then turn off the left nitro-blaster in three . . . two . . . one . . . NOW, MAVERICK!"

Maverick shut down the rocket on his left side, and just when it looked like they were going to crash, they whipped into a tight arc. The right blaster shot them around the turn, missing Dug's front bumper by inches. Jimmy hit the blue button again. The right nitro-blaster shut down, leaving Maverick perfectly lined up on the track.

"Wow!" said Jimmy, a little dazed.

Grandpa appeared on the Cabcom screen, a huge smile hanging under his white mustache. "Jimmy, you did it! You did it, my boy." Jimmy could see him dancing a little jig. "You wouldn't believe what the commentators are saying about you. They reckon that's the best move they've seen in years."

Jimmy's chest swelled with pride, but he knew that he still had lots to do.

"How are you holding up, Maverick?" he asked his robot racer.

"Ha!" Maverick laughed. "Never been better. I was amazing. And Jimmy, you weren't too bad either. That was brilliant!"

As he looked down the long, straight track in front of them, Jimmy eased his grip on the steering wheel a little. Far ahead, he could see Monster trundling along, kicking up dirt and dust. His next job was to overtake Missy, but he had just noticed something else...

"Maverick —"

"That's how we roll, Jimmy baby! Robot-racer style!"

"Maverick, look!"

"If I had hands, I'd give you a high five!"

"Maverick, look out!" Jimmy wrenched the wheel to the right as they drove straight toward another thick section of vines. Maverick's tires screeched as they avoided the vines. Jimmy flicked the wheel back to keep them safely on the road.

"That was close," Jimmy said.

"Oops," said Maverick, his electronic voice sounding embarrassed. "I got carried away and stopped paying attention for a second."

Jimmy smiled. "That's okay. It was pretty awesome."

Up ahead, the brake lights on Missy's truck were brightly shining.

"What is she doing?" Jimmy asked Maverick.

But when they got closer, they figured it out. The track had narrowed so much that Monster's massive wheels barely fit on the road. On either side of the track was a swamp, with overhanging trees making it seem dark and creepy. With no room to pass on either side of the monster truck, Jimmy had no choice but to slow down to a crawl behind Missy. He had to wait for a chance to overtake her.

"Come on!" said Maverick. "Can't we honk at her? It always worked when I was a taxi."

"Did it?"

"Well, no, but it made me feel better. What about the swamp? It can't be that deep. Don't forget, we've got the floating device."

Jimmy glanced at the murky water on either side of the track. He was just about to agree and drive into the swamp when he saw a ripple on the surface and lots of tiny flashes of white light.

"Maverick, can we get the Internet on the Cabcom?" Jimmy asked.

"This is no time to check your email," said Maverick. But he fired up the Cabcom so it came up with the official Robot Races website.

"Search 'wildlife,'" Jimmy said.

The screen displayed some options of pages to look at. It showed the different places around the world that Robot Races took place. "Choose 'Amazon swamps,'" he said. A page of information popped up. "Activate speech."

The Cabcom burst into life. A woman's voice filled the cab, reading the information that was displayed on the screen, leaving Jimmy to steer.

"The swamps of the Amazon jungle are filled with dangerous animals. The most deadly are probably the great electric eels. The swamps are their natural habitat, and they feed off tiny fishes and insects. If disturbed they can emit powerful charges of electricity."

"Hmm, so that's what those flashes are," said Jimmy. "They're from giant electric eels! Hundreds of them, by the look of it. Even if we managed to float across there, one false move and the eels would attack."

The voice on the Cabcom continued. "The eels hunt in packs. Combined, they could generate enough electrical charge to power a city."

"In other words," said Jimmy, "they'd fry your motherboard."

Maverick was unusually quiet for a moment. "Yikes," he said eventually.

"But you're right," Jimmy said, staring at Monster's bumper. "We can't just sit here. What else have you got?"

Maverick ran though his upgrades, but there didn't seem to be anything that would help. "I'll activate the headlights," he said. "These overhanging trees make it so dark out there."

"The trees! That's it! We can overtake easily!" said Jimmy with a new energy. "We can use the grappling hooks to grab hold of the trees!"

"Of course!" said Maverick, catching onto the idea. "I can winch us in so fast that we'll sail through the air and land on the other side of

Missy and Monster! Why didn't I think of that? I'm supposed to be the brains of this operation."

"Very funny," Jimmy said. Then he imagined the scene and what they would need to do. "Leapfrogging a monster truck could work, but it will be dangerous."

"I like it," Maverick said, sounding excited. "We'd be jumping — actually jumping — into first place!" Maverick sounded excited. "It's a genius idea, Jimmy. Let's do it!"

CHAPTER 8
A RISKY MOVE

Jimmy knew what he had to do. He tightened his seat belt and closed his eyes. "Let's go."

"Yes!" said Maverick. "Deploying grappling hooks." A compartment on the hood slid open. The hooks raised up like missiles getting ready to launch. "Identifying target."

Maverick's sensors quickly mapped the area and found the perfect tree to target. It was a strong one with a branch that extended out over the track. If this was going to work, that branch had to be really strong.

"Go for it, Maverick!" said Jimmy. "FIRE!"

The hook fired, sending more birds and wildlife scattering. It bounced off the branch, and Maverick quickly reeled it in. "Shoot! I'll adjust the elevation," he said.

Just then, Jimmy heard a sound from behind him. He looked to see Dug coming up fast. If they waited much longer, every one of the racers would catch up.

"Maverick, we need to go now!" he said.

"Okay! Ready . . . aim . . . fire!"

Jimmy pressed the button. The hook flew up again, sailing over the monster truck and biting deep into a thick, broad branch.

"Here we go!" Maverick shouted.

"Whoa!" shouted Jimmy, surprised at how quickly they left the ground. They swung through the air like Tarzan, gaining speed, the branch creaking under their weight. Just when they reached the halfway point, Jimmy looked down at the top of Monster and the swamp on either side of her, which was flashing with angry electric eels.

"Preparing to cut cable," said Maverick.

Jimmy panicked.

"What? You never said anything about cutting anything!"

"It's the only way, Jimmy. Trust me!"

Jimmy held onto the steering wheel for dear life as a blade cut through the tough steel coil. For a moment, Maverick and Jimmy hung in midair above the track and the swamp, nothing supporting them. Jimmy felt as if they were floating, and for a second everything was peaceful and quiet. Until, that is, gravity took hold and they began to drop.

Maverick was still moving forward, the swing of the rope having done its job. Jimmy yelled out loud as they sailed through the air with all the grace and beauty of a flying brick.

"Waaaaagh!"

WHOMP! They landed with a hard bump on the track, directly ahead of a confused-looking Missy.

"Woooo-hooooo!" cheered Maverick with a huge smile on his face.

Jimmy had to do some smart steering so they didn't drive into the swamp. Once he had Maverick under control, he pressed the accelerator hard. They sped off down the track. They raced past the swamp and out into the jungle, where the track spread out a little and they were really able to pick up speed.

"Don't you ever do that again!" shouted Jimmy.

"Sorry, I should have warned you about cutting that cable. But look —" Maverick turned on the official Robot Races tracking system, a map of the course with small colored dots showing the positions of the competitors. "We're in first place!"

Jimmy looked. Sure enough, there was their small blue dot in front. Missy behind in second place, and Dug and Lightning still somewhere in the swamp. Sammy and Kako were close behind them. Strangely, Jimmy couldn't see Horace and Zoom on the map at all.

"Okay," said Jimmy. "You were lucky."

"I was a genius."

"Whatever!" Jimmy laughed.

Grandpa's face appeared on the Cabcom. "You're in first place!" he announced.

"We know!" said Jimmy and Maverick together.

"Good job, boys! The commentators are calling it the craziest move in the history of Robot Races!" Jimmy was strangely proud of that. "You obviously don't need my help, which is just as well. The airship is coming to take the parents and technicians to the base camp for the night. You'll be there in no time. We can repair and refuel there."

"And eat! I could eat a horse!" said Jimmy.

Grandpa laughed. "I don't know about a horse, but I've got a sack of cabbages from That's Shallot! we can dive into."

Yuck! thought Jimmy.

In the background of the picture, Jimmy could see the other teams talking to their racers on headsets.

Mr. Pelly was talking to Horace in a quiet voice. Omar Bahur was barking instructions to Samir so loudly that Jimmy could hear him clearly, even if he couldn't understand what he was saying. Grandpa leaned into the camera, his wrinkly face and white hair filling the screen. Jimmy couldn't help but smile.

"Between you and me, I think old Mr. Pelly is up to something. As well as that fancy laser navigation system Zoom's got, he's also been feeding Horace information all day, looking at old maps and charts. Some of them are ancient. They must be from when the first explorers landed here."

"Hmm, that is strange," said Jimmy, remembering that Zoom had been missing from the tracking system map earlier. "Keep an eye on him, will you, Grandpa? See you at the camp."

"Will do. Over and out!"

Jimmy finally relaxed and sped up, confident that no one was going to catch them for the rest of the day. Everyone had gotten stuck behind Missy in the swamp, and Maverick was now in the lead by miles. He sat back, put Maverick into cruise control, and whistled a happy tune. He couldn't believe his luck!

WOOOOOOSH!

Jimmy grabbed the wheel and continued steering as something whizzed past them. He looked over to see a sleek black robot car fly past him at an alarming speed. Jimmy couldn't believe his eyes, but it was true.

They had just been overtaken by Horace and Zoom!

CHAPTER 9
A RACE BETWEEN RIVALS

"Impossible!" said Maverick, after his robot recognition software had confirmed who had passed them. "They came out of nowhere!"

"Maverick, did we go the right way? How did they get ahead of us?" Jimmy asked.

"I don't know. I'm the best navigator there is, and I can't work out how they did it!"

Jimmy sped up again, trying to catch Zoom at the next turn. There was no time to sit back and relax anymore. The race had just gotten interesting again!

"They must have found a shortcut!" Jimmy shook his head, refusing to believe it. The rumor

was that track builders put a hidden shortcut
in every race. If you found it, you could skip a
whole section, which could mean the difference
between first place and last. But in the entire
time that Jimmy had been watching the races,
no racer had ever found one. No one really
knew whether Lord Leadpipe put them in when
he designed the tracks or if they were just a
Robot Races myth.

"Maybe Horace found a shortcut using his
fancy laser guidance system." Jimmy thumped
the steering wheel in frustration.

"Ow!" said Maverick.

"Sorry." Jimmy patted Maverick's dashboard.

They took the turn and the track widened.
Maverick started to overtake, but Zoom
matched his speed. Jimmy glanced over to see
Horace in the driver's seat, smiling and waving
sarcastically. He reached out a finger and pressed
something on his dashboard.

"Ouch!" yelled Maverick, lurching to the
side. Jimmy looked out the window to see
what had happened. Flamethrowers had

suddenly appeared from the middle of Zoom's wheels, sending huge yellow jets of fire toward Maverick. The flames reached out and nearly touched his tires. Jimmy could feel the heat from the driver's seat.

"HOTHOTHOTHOT!" shouted Maverick.

"Let's drop back!" ordered Jimmy. "The tree canopy is so thick around here that the race organizers won't be able to see Horace cheating."

"No, I can take it," Maverick said. "This is our race. We can't let him bully us."

Jimmy didn't object any more, but he could smell the unmistakable stench of burning rubber from Maverick's wheels as the tires heated up. He kept Maverick to the far side of the track and away from the flames. He didn't have much room before he would be pushed off the edge. If the flames got any closer, the tires could set on fire and explode.

The Cabcom bleeped, and the screen was filled with Horace Pelly's tanned face.

"Afternoon, losers!" he said.

"Turn off the flamethrowers, Horace!" Jimmy demanded.

"Oh, is that what that button does?" Horace laughed. "Give up, then," he ordered.

"No chance!" shouted Jimmy. "I don't take orders from cheats like you, Pelly!"

Horace's face dropped into a scowl. "My laser guidance system is perfectly within the rules. I'm surprised That's Shallot! didn't buy you a new one. I hear you're helping their business tremendously at the moment. People just look at you and say, 'What a lemon!'"

Horace laughed like a hyena, and Jimmy hit the Cabcom screen to make him disappear. The track led them toward a clearing in the forest. Jimmy was determined to get there first. But when Horace saw that Jimmy wasn't going to drop back, he redirected all power to Zoom's engines. The flamethrowers went out, and the sleek black robot powered forward toward the clearing.

They were still neck and neck as Jimmy saw the clearing ahead. Rising up in the center of the

open space was a gigantic stone statue. It looked
like the totem poles that he had read about at
school. He guessed it must have been put there
by an ancient civilization that had once lived in
the jungle. Totem poles were meant to scare off
evil spirits, and at the moment Jimmy wished
this one could get rid of Horace Pelly.

Both robots roared into the open. Jimmy
was surprised when Zoom veered to one side,
choosing not to take the most direct line across
the clearing.

"This is our chance, Jimmy!" said Maverick

"Are you sure? Why isn't Zoom going that
way?" Jimmy asked.

"We don't have time to argue! Go for it!"

Jimmy dropped back and overtook Zoom
on the other side, edging around him. He could
have sworn he saw Horace smirk. Then Horace
grabbed Zoom's controls, gripping the steering
wheel. He threw his robot racer to the right.
Zoom lurched right, the strong black metal
exterior crunching as it hit Maverick.

"Ow!" said Maverick as he lurched to one

side. "He rammed us!" Just as he tried to recover, Zoom hit them once more, sending them toward the ancient stone monument.

"Brace for impact!" said Maverick. Jimmy tensed, grabbing the seat, waiting for the crash as they hit the old totem pole.

But the crash never came. Instead, Jimmy felt the ground in front of the monument give way. He saw the trees around him rush upward. His stomach jumped like he was in a fast-dropping elevator.

"Whoa!" Maverick yelled as his safety airbags exploded open and they hit the ground with a jolt. They had fallen right into a trap!

CHAPTER 10
CAUGHT IN A TRAP

"Jimmy? Jimmy? Are you okay?" Jimmy heard Maverick say. It was pitch black, and he couldn't see his hand in front of his face.

"Jimmy!" Maverick yelled more urgently.

"Yeah, I'm okay," gasped Jimmy finally.

The fall had knocked the breath out of him. He struggled to fill his lungs. Jimmy sat still for a few more moments, checking himself over. He had bashed his head against Maverick's door and could feel a small bump developing. His ears were ringing slightly, but Jimmy knew that it could have been much worse. The airbag and seat belt had saved him from a much nastier injury. He had bitten into his lip in the crash. His mouth now tasted like blood. Otherwise he was all right — just a little shaken up.

"Are you okay, Maverick?" Jimmy asked as he opened Maverick's door and stepped out shakily. He stretched, making sure all of his body parts worked, coughing out the dust that was settling around him.

"Me? I'm fine. My fenders are damaged and the only working nitro-blaster fell off when we fell. Other than that, I'm fine. Good thing your grandpa doesn't skimp on safety devices," said Maverick.

"I know," replied Jimmy. "That was a close call."

"Are you sure you're okay? That was still quite a fall for a human to take."

"Yeah, I'll be fine. Thanks for looking after me, Maverick," Jimmy patted his racer.

"No problem, partner," the robot replied. "All part of the service."

Jimmy looked up to where sunlight poured in through a hole in the roof high above him.

A shadow appeared, and for a brief moment Jimmy thought it might be a safetybot. His heart sank. If he and Maverick had to be rescued, they'd be out of the race!

Jimmy was almost relieved when he heard Horace's smug voice.

"Did you have a little fall?" said Horace. "You really should be more careful."

"Get us out of here, Horace!" Jimmy demanded.

"Tut-tut! You didn't say the magic word. Never mind, I'm not going to help you anyway." Horace walked around the edge of the hole like a proud peacock. "It was Dad who found these secret chambers. He had been studying old explorers' maps from hundreds of years ago. He came across an ancient temple buried below the stone monument. Even the track builders hadn't found it, so it'll be ages before the safetybots come to get you out."

Jimmy balled his hands into fists, feeling ready to burst. Horace had been planning this all along.

"You won't get away with this, Horace! Get me out now!"

Horace Pelly laughed, and it echoed all the way down to Jimmy. "Sorry, Jimmy. I don't take orders from losers. See ya!"

He strolled away from the edge of the hole. Jimmy heard him laughing as he drove away in Zoom.

"What are we going to do, Maverick?"

"The Cabcom was damaged in the fall." Maverick sighed. "I'll keep trying to fix it, but I think we might just have to wait for rescue."

Jimmy walked over to a pillar and placed his hand on it. It was ridged and bumpy, and Jimmy used what little light there was to see that it was covered in painstakingly carved ancient symbols. So were the walls and the dusty floor.

"Dark, isn't it?" said Maverick. "I'd make some light, but my headlights cracked in the fall."

"Jimmy, Maverick, are you receiving me? Over." Grandpa's voice was coming from the dashboard. He sounded worried. Jimmy dashed back into the driver's seat and looked at the Cabcom, which fizzled and crackled.

"Grandpa, I can hear you! Can you get help?" Jimmy could see the old man's face on the screen, but there was no reply. Until —

"Jimmy? Maverick?" said Grandpa's worried voice. He frowned at the screen and appeared to hit the camera he was staring into. "It's no good, I've lost them again!" they heard him say.

"He can't hear us. Maverick, can you contact him another way?"

"Sorry, Jimmy, this is the best I can do." Maverick gave a deep sigh.

"Pelly!" shouted Grandpa on the screen, turning to face Horace's dad. "What has your boy done to my grandson? They were neck and neck, and now Jimmy has disappeared!"

"What on earth are you accusing me of?" asked Mr. Pelly. Grandpa stood up and threw down his headset, but he was shouting so loud that Jimmy could still hear him. Another voice joined in, the familiar sound of Joshua Johnson, the Robot Coordinator.

"Gentlemen, sit down! Fighting won't solve anything!"

"We'll see about that!" There was a scuffle offscreen. The picture flickered and faded, just as it looked like Grandpa was going to get very angry indeed.

"They sound like they're having fun," said Jimmy with a sigh. He tried hard to think of the best thing to do, struggling not to think about the fact that they could be trapped in this dark, cold tomb forever. It would have been very easy to panic and curl up into a whimpering little ball, but there was one thing worse that being stuck: Horace Pelly winning.

"This is our race," he said.

"Pardon?" Maverick replied.

"This is *our* race," Jimmy repeated, with more confidence. "We were winning. And no one is going to take it away from us, especially not him."

With a steady look in his eye, he climbed onto the roof of Maverick. He jumped up and down, attempting to make the leap to the ground above them. It was useless. It was far too high to jump. He took a deep breath and thought hard.

"Maverick, do we still have a second grappling hook?"

"Yes."

"Excellent. Shoot for the edge of the hole above. You can pull us out. Then we can contact Grandpa."

"Great plan, Jimmy!"

Maverick engaged the grappling hook and it rose out of his hood. He fired, but the first few shots landed wide of the mark, hitting the temple wall uselessly. On the fourth attempt, the hook flew out toward the sky. When they reeled it in slowly, they found the sharp spikes could not get a grip. Instead it just brought soil down on top of them from the edge of the hole as it crumbled away some more. The hook fell to the floor with a depressing clang.

"It's no use," said Jimmy.

He sat down on the floor, resting against Maverick's side. For a moment, he was angry with Grandpa. He was supposed to be the robotic genius with a plan for everything. Where was their upgrade for this situation?

He hit his head back against the door in frustration, bashing the ridiculous cartoon onion with the words "That's Shallot! proudly sponsors Jimmy and Maverick" underneath. Why had they been so stupid to accept sponsorship from them? What could a fruit and veggie supplier do that could help them in the race?

Suddenly Jimmy was hit by an idea. It was so obvious that he could have kicked himself. He shot up with a grin.

"Carrots!" he yelled.

"What?" Maverick asked.

"We've been so silly! We've got the night-time vision upgrade from our sponsors. Maverick, engage Carrot Vision!"

Jimmy quickly picked up the nitro-blaster that lay on the ground next to Maverick, and laid it carefully behind his seat. He remembered how delicate Grandpa had said it could be. He certainly remembered the large burn mark on the ceiling of the shed! He wanted to keep the blaster, just in case Grandpa could fix it later. Then he climbed into the driver's seat, and Maverick turned the Carrot Vision on. A visor rose up from the hood, covering the windshield. The whole chamber seemed to be bathed in a green glow, and suddenly they could see everything.

"Wow! Carrots really can help you see in the dark!" said Maverick.

Now that they had the visor, they could see how big the chamber was. The walls and floor were covered in carvings. Some of the marks were in an ancient language that even Maverick, with his language-translator chip, couldn't understand. Some were pretty designs, but others were larger and scarier: a mythical beast that was half-man, half-panther; a ferocious winged ape with teeth and claws the size of Jimmy's head; and a fish with razor-sharp fins, leaping out of the water, its eyes glinting in the green light.

"Jimmy?" said Maverick. "What are they?"

"Gods, maybe," he guessed. He had once watched a documentary on this sort of thing with Grandpa. "The people here used to worship them, and probably bring them sacrifices. Why are you shaking?"

Maverick's engine was shuddering so hard that the broken fender was performing a tap dance on the ground outside. Jimmy felt like he was sitting on a washing machine on the spin cycle.

"Because I don't like the look of that one!"

Jimmy turned to see the biggest carving of them all, completely filling an entire wall. It was an enormous cobra with little images of people running away from it at the bottom of the wall. Around the huge cobra drawing were dozens of smaller snake carvings.

"Do you think he thinks we're one of his sacrifices?" said Maverick with a gulp.

Jimmy didn't like the look of it either, but tried to keep calm. He searched the chamber until he found something. "Look down there!" he said suddenly.

Maverick let out a burst of smoke from his exhaust pipe. "What? Where? Is it the Snake God? I don't see anything!" he panicked.

"Exactly! The chamber just goes on and on. If we drive down there we might find an exit."

"Anything to get us out of here!" Maverick said, sounding much more like his old self again.

Jimmy slammed his door shut. Maverick started his engine, and they slowly drove into the dark.

They edged along the chamber, wary of any weak floors or ceilings. If they had managed to fall through a ceiling in the clearing, then the rest of the chamber could fall in at any moment. Maverick was shaking a little less now, happy to be away from the image of the Snake God, and was talking quickly.

"It's just the way they move, you know? I don't trust them, the horrible slithery things. And I don't like the way they poke their tongues out like that. It's just rude, that's what it is."

"I'm sure we'll be safer down here," said Jimmy.

"Sorry I got you into this," said Maverick. "I shouldn't have told you to cut across that clearing. We would have been all right if we had kept to the path like you said. Now we're stuck."

"Don't be silly. We're a team, and we stick together. Horace led us to a trap, and he pushed us into it. No one is to blame except him."

"True!" said Maverick, sounding even more like his old chirpy, cheery self. "Let's concentrate on getting out of here!"

But they hadn't gone more than a few feet when they heard a huge crash and an explosion behind them.

"What the . . .?" Jimmy exclaimed as the ground shook behind him. He looked around to see thousands of tons of stone and dirt falling from the roof as the ruins seemed to crumble around him. A cloud of dust swept toward him, and rocks the size of baseballs hurtled toward Maverick's windows.

"Watch out!" yelled Jimmy. "The roof's falling in!"

CHAPTER 11
DEEPER UNDERGROUND

"Are you all right?" Jimmy said when the noise of the explosion had stopped.

"Well, I'm going to need a new paint job, if that's what you mean," Maverick joked. "And it's going to take your grandpa hours to get out all these cracks on my glasswork."

"I'll take that as a yes," said Jimmy, smiling at Maverick's reply. "It sounded like the rock fall came from that chamber we just left. Let's go and check it out."

Maverick did a quick handbrake turn so he was facing the other way. Jimmy poked his head out of the door, peering into the darkness. He couldn't make out what had happened, so he sat back down and looked through the Carrot Vision visor.

"Maverick, can you zoom in on that rock fall? I can't see that far."

"Sure thing! Zooming in now."

The picture on the visor became larger. Jimmy was able to understand what he was looking at. At the end of the chamber, in a cloud of dust and broken rocks, was a large hovercraft covered in soil and debris from the fall. It had fallen down in almost the exact same spot as Maverick had earlier. It had brought down another large chunk of the jungle floor with it.

"It's Maximus!" said Jimmy. "Sammy must be in there. Let's go and help."

Maverick rushed to the hoverbot. Sammy climbed out of his cockpit, shaken and scared.

"Jimmy? Where am I?" he said, looking dazed and confused.

"An old temple, we think. I'll explain later. Are you hurt?" He shook his head. "And Maximus?"

Maximus said something in Arabic, and Sammy translated. "His spare fuel tank has cracked, but there is no damage to the rest of him. Thankfully, the hovercraft's air cushions softened our fall. I was crossing the clearing when my father ordered me to go close to the stone monument to save time. It looked dangerous, but —"

He was interrupted by the Cabcom blaring from Maximus's cockpit, where Omar was shouting at the top of his voice, "Samir! Answer me immediately!"

The Cabcom hissed and went blank as it lost its signal. Sammy actually looked relieved. Then the walls shuddered again, and another bucketful of soil landed on top of Maximus.

"We've got to get out of here," said Jimmy.

"Yes. It is creepy," said Sammy.

Jimmy laughed. "It's also falling down. There might be an escape route down this way."

The hole crumbled some more, and another large chunk of rock fell down. It just missed Maverick and Maximus, then rolled across the floor and struck one of the carved pillars that supported the ceiling. The pillar cracked, a small line appearing in the carvings that wound their way up to the roof.

"Uh-oh," said Maverick.

"Let's go!" said Jimmy. "Move, move, move!"

Both boys hopped back into their robots. The motors on the robots roared as they tried to make a quick getaway. The pillar cracked and crumbled. Then with a great crash, it fell to the floor, leaving the roof unsupported.

"Full throttle, Maverick!" yelled Jimmy.

"You don't have to tell me twice!"

Maverick and Maximus zipped along the underground tunnel, away from the crumbling hole. The roof and supporting walls fell in on each other with a loud crash, sending stone and dust flying. As they sped along trying to outrun the cloud of dust and rubble that chased them, Jimmy spotted a section of wall ahead that had a gap in it. At the last second he steered into it, Maximus following just behind. The tunnel was small, and Maximus was so large that he just fit into it. The two racers sped along as fast as they could, as the ceiling caved in behind them.

They slowed down, safe for the moment.

"There goes the rest of the roof," said Jimmy. "I just hope this tunnel leads to an exit, or we're trapped!"

The roof and wall of the tunnel seemed more stable than the main chamber and unlikely to cave in, so they slowed down a little more, Maximus following behind. Jimmy's Cabcom lit up, and Sammy's voice came from the speakers.

"It is good thing we can use the Cabcom shortwave radio to talk to each other, yes?" he said. "Where should we go now?"

Jimmy thought that Sammy sounded quite perky, even happy. He might have said that he was enjoying this, if their lives hadn't been at stake.

"I haven't a clue. We'll just have to see where this takes us."

They continued along the dark passageway for a while.

"How are you feeling, Maverick?"

"Awful," moaned the robot. "My sensors keep picking up snakes in the area."

"Don't be silly. We are way underground."

"My sensors don't lie, Jimmy. There's a horrible hissing sound coming from somewhere nearby."

"It's impossible. This place hasn't been used in thousands of years! Just take it easy."

Maverick seemed to calm down a little. "You're right. I'm being silly. There's no way that there would be — EEK!"

Maverick slammed on his brakes, and a screech of rubber filled the air. Maximus ground to a halt behind him, reversing his thrusters so he didn't crash into Maverick.

Jimmy peered ahead and saw the reason for Maverick's sudden maneuver. The floor dropped in front of them, leaving no way past. It left a pit in the floor, filled with hundreds of thin, wriggling, slithery, slimy —

"SNAKES!" wailed Maverick.

There were vipers of all different colors moving over each other and hissing hungrily.

"Maverick, calm down!" Jimmy said, not feeling too calm himself.

It was no good. Just like at the press conference, the robot started to shudder and twitch, his hood starting to steam as he overheated.

"Get them away!" he yelled, and started to reverse, but Maximus was in the way. In Maximus's cockpit, Sammy looked very confused. Jimmy hit the Cabcom.

"What's the matter?" said Sammy.

"Maverick's freaking out! Can you back up?" Maximus's reversing light pinged on, but before they could even move, Maverick tried to turn in the cramped space.

"Maverick, no!" Jimmy shouted. He could see there was no room to turn, and the robot's nose swung into the wall beside them.

Instead of the expected crunch of metal, however, there was a sharp click. The carving that Maverick had bumped into sank into the wall like a light switch being turned on. But no light appeared. Jimmy turned in his seat as he heard a scraping sound. He saw a giant stone slowly roll into place at the end of the tunnel, cutting off the tunnel just behind Maximus. The two boys and two robots were now well and truly stuck in the tight space. And the tunnel was silent, except for the sound of hissing from the pit at the end.

"We are trapped?" said Sammy.

"Yes," said Jimmy. "It would seem so."

"Sorry," said Maverick. "I just really don't like snakes."

"Don't worry, Maverick," said Jimmy, patting the dashboard. "We'll find a way out. We have plenty of time."

As soon as he said the words, Jimmy knew he would regret them. First he heard a squeaking noise. Then the corridor was filled with the sound of stone scraping on stone. Jimmy looked to the side of the tunnel and saw what he had feared. The carvings on either side were getting closer.

The walls were closing in!

CHAPTER 12
TIME TO ESCAPE

It was happening slowly, but Jimmy was sure of it. The walls on either side of them were getting closer and closer.

"Sammy! It's a trap! It must be to protect the temple. We've got to get out!" yelled Jimmy.

Maximus said something on the Cabcom, and Sammy translated. "Maximus has calculated that we have five minutes at the current speed before the robots start to get crushed," he said. He sounded surprisingly calm.

"What do we do?" asked Jimmy. He was starting to panic now.

"Whoever built this would have put in an emergency stop button to stop themselves from being crushed," Sammy told him. "We just have to find it."

He got out of his cockpit. Maximus flooded the small space with light. Jimmy followed. They desperately searched the walls for a button. They pushed on everything they could find.

Within a minute or so, they had been down the whole tunnel. The walls were still closing in.

"There is nothing else to push," said Jimmy.

"Don't be so sure," said Sammy.

Sammy was staring at a small ledge on the other side of the viper pit. On the wall there was a carving of a puma. Its nose seemed to glisten in the light.

"You can't be serious," said Jimmy. "There's no way we can get past the pit."

"Oh, I don't like this at all," muttered Maverick.

Sammy shrugged. "It's worth a try."

Before Jimmy could stop him, Sammy had launched himself across the pit. His feet flew just above the hissing snakes. A huge viper snapped upward, its deadly fangs slicing the air just inches from Sammy's feet. Sammy calmly landed on the other side of the pit.

"See? It's no big deal." Sammy reached out and touched the puma's nose.

There was a loud click and the walls shook to a stop.

"Nice one, Sammy. You did it!" But just as Jimmy finished his sentence, a second loud click echoed around the temple. Then the walls began to move again, but this time they were moving twice as fast.

"That was not part of the plan," Sammy said uncertainly. He gave the nose another tap, but the button was now locked in place and wouldn't budge.

"Sammy, it didn't work. Get back over, quick!"

Sammy launched himself across the pit again. He flew through the air above the angry snakes. This time his foot landed on the very edge of the pit, and he slipped. His foot slid down toward the snakes. He gave a small yell as he realized what was happening.

Jimmy dived forward, reaching for Sammy's hand. For a moment, he thought he wasn't going to make it. But his sweaty palm found Sammy's, and the two boys gripped each other desperately.

"Hold on," Jimmy said through gritted teeth. He could feel his hand slipping. Sammy's eyes were wide with panic. Jimmy thrust his free hand forward and reached for Sammy's other arm. He managed to grasp onto his other wrist, getting a better hold on him.

For a moment, they dangled above the viper pit. The snakes below hissed, and the giant viper jumped up again. This time it sunk its teeth deep into Sammy's shoe.

"Aaaah!" yelled Sammy in desperation. He shook his foot, causing the snake to hiss even more dangerously. He shook it again, harder this time, and the huge snake finally let go.

Jimmy gripped tighter and pulled his friend to safety. They both collapsed onto the floor.

"Are you okay?" Jimmy asked urgently. "You've been bitten."

"I think I am," Sammy replied, inspecting his shoe. "The snake bit only the shoe and not my foot. But we will both be dead if we don't get out of here fast."

"It's no use," said Jimmy.

Sammy actually laughed. "Is this the famous British spirit? I thought you chaps never surrendered!"

Jimmy was stunned. He couldn't believe that the boy who was always so serious could laugh at a time like this. The moment that his father wasn't around, Sammy became a different person. He was funny, confident, daring, and quick thinking.

Sammy seemed to stare off into the distance for a moment. He appeared calm, in spite of the moving walls. Then after a moment he shouted, "Wait! I see something."

He yelled an instruction to Maximus in Arabic, and the hoverbot killed the lights, plunging them into darkness. "Look."

Jimmy wasn't sure where he should look in the pitch black, but it soon became clear. High up on the wall at the end of the tunnel was a tiny speck of light.

"Daylight!" he shouted. "We can escape!"

"Yes, if only we could open that hole wide enough to drive out."

Jimmy had an idea. "I have just the thing!"

Maximus lit up the corridor again. Jimmy hurriedly searched Maverick. He came out holding the nitro-blaster that had been knocked off Maverick's side earlier in the race.

"It's blasting time!"

"Will it blow us an escape route?" said Sammy, his face full of hope.

"It should. I didn't use all of the fuel in this blaster yet."

Maximus said something in Arabic, and Jimmy was pretty sure it wasn't good news.

"He says we have two minutes," translated Sammy. "Let's do it."

Jimmy stood on Sammy's shoulders, steadying himself against the wall. He attached the nitro-blaster to it near the small chunk of sunlight. He used some strong tape that Grandpa had left in Maverick's trunk.

"Will it do it?" Sammy asked.

"I don't see why not," said Jimmy. "Grandpa's got a knack for blowing things up."

"One minute!" said Sammy. They looked at the side walls, which were frighteningly close. They were already touching the rubber air cushions that kept Maximus hovering. Even the super-cool Egyptian robot sounded worried as he gave a countdown to the moment when they would be squeezed like a lemon.

"Thirty seconds!" Sammy took cover in Maximus, and Jimmy dived into Maverick.

"Maverick, will this work?" he whispered.

"I've patched into the nitro-blaster's remote sensor so that I can detonate from here. It should make short work of that wall, but there is no way to tell if it was damaged in the fall or not," said Maverick. "There's only one way to find out."

"Ten! Nine! Eight! Seven!"

"Here we go!" Jimmy pressed the button that was flashing and dived for cover. There was a horrible pause when Jimmy thought the blaster wasn't going to work, and then —

KABOOM!

The nitro-blaster activated. The explosion sprayed chunks of rock and dust down onto them. Without giving the dust a chance to settle, Jimmy floored the accelerator and headed straight for where he hoped a hole was.

"Whhhoooaaa," he yelled as he felt Maverick flying over the rubble. The next thing he knew, he was being blinded by the bright light of a jungle clearing.

As Jimmy's eyes adjusted to the daylight, he heard the loud whirring of a giant fan. Maximus shot out of the temple. Moments later there was another rumbling noise from inside. The two walls crashed together, blocking the exit they had just made.

"Woo-hoo!" cheered Jimmy. "That was amazing! I can't believe it actually worked! Amazing! "

Sammy got out of his cockpit. "What a relief!"

They slapped their hands together. "Sammy, I never would have made it out of there without you. If you hadn't kept calm and noticed that gap, Maverick and I would be totally flat right now."

"But we would have been stuck if you had not had that nitro thing." Sammy grinned. "This is teamwork, yes?"

Just then there was a crackling noise from inside Maverick. The Cabcom had started to work again. The two boys squeezed into Maverick. Grandpa's worried, sweating, white-mustached face popped onto the screen.

"There you are! Oh, thank goodness! And Sammy too! Are you safe?"

"We are now!" grinned Jimmy.

"Although my bodywork has seen better days!" chipped in Maverick.

Jimmy launched into an explanation of what had happened, and where they had been for the last few hours. Sammy enthusiastically helped fill in the exciting parts. When they had finished, Grandpa wiped his brow and looked exhausted, like he'd been through the whole ordeal himself.

"I'm just glad you're both okay. I've been worried sick."

"Mr. Roberts," said Sammy. "Is my father there?"

Grandpa looked around and turned back to the camera, a bit embarrassed. "He, er . . . he went off to get dinner."

Sammy looked shocked. "He is not worried?"

"He sounded more angry actually," said Grandpa. "I'll tell him what happened and that you're all right."

Sammy went quiet.

"Are you at the overnight camp? Save us some dinner!" Jimmy joked, trying to change the subject to cheer his friend up.

Grandpa shook his head sadly. "Sorry, Jimmy. The race rules state you must start on day two from the exact same spot that you stopped at. That means that you'll have to stay put overnight."

Jimmy and Sammy exchanged a look.

"Right here? In the jungle?" Sammy asked.

"In the dark? With the creepy crawlies?" Jimmy said, trying to sound brave.

"Don't worry, boys, you'll be fine," said Grandpa. "Just whatever you do, don't —"

The screen popped and went dead. Grandpa's face disappeared, leaving Sammy and Jimmy alone in the dark with the sound of the jungle growing louder and louder and louder . . .

CHAPTER 13
CAMPFIRE TALES

"We're alone," said Jimmy. "In the jungle."

"With no camping supplies," said Sammy.

"And lots of wild animals and insects," said Maverick.

The three of them crept closer to each other. Maximus muttered something.

"What did he say?" asked Jimmy.

"He said, 'Pull yourselves together,'" said Sammy. "And he's right."

After searching through Maverick's trunk, Sammy and Jimmy found a few useful things. There was a large tent canopy that Grandpa had packed in case he needed to fix Maverick in the rain. There were even two sleeping bags and bottles of water. Grandpa had packed everything! There was also a packet of Grandpa's favorite marshmallows and some trail mix from That's Shallot!

Sammy didn't have any emergency gear. He explained that his father did not believe in emergencies. He preferred to keep Maximus's weight low in order to make him faster.

Jimmy happily shared his things with Sammy. They set up the tent, stretching it between Maximus and some trees as shelter. As it grew dark, they sat on logs and lit a fire so that they could toast marshmallows.

Maverick had parked alongside Maximus, and the two were chatting away in Arabic. Maverick was using his built-in translation chip. Jimmy couldn't be sure, but he thought that Maverick was boring Maximus with stories of celebrities he had given a ride to when he had been a regular taxi.

"You and Maverick seem to get along together well. You talk like friends," said Sammy.

Jimmy shrugged. "I suppose we do. Grandpa programmed him, so I suppose Maverick's just like him. We disagree sometimes, though. What about you and Maximus?"

Sammy looked down at his marshmallow. "Father says you should not be friends with a robot," he said sadly. "I should be his master, not his friend."

Jimmy chugged some water. "Sammy, do you like being a robot racer?"

Sammy did not answer for a long while. "It has always been my father's dream for me to be a Robot Races champion," he said at last.

"And what about you?" Jimmy asked.

"It is my dream too," said Sammy quickly. "But Father knows what I should do in a race, and I do not."

He looked sad. Jimmy quickly tried to cheer him up.

"You know exactly what you need to do. You knew how to get us out of the temple, didn't you? And how to set up the camp?" Sammy nodded. "And you enjoyed every second!"

Sammy laughed. "Yes, very much."

"So when you haven't got your dad shouting orders at you, you're a brilliant racer."

Sammy let Jimmy's words sink in. "Father only cares about the race." He took a bite of his hot marshmallow and raised the stick he had used to toast it like a sword. "I will show him. I can be a real racer." He sat up straight and tall, determined.

After a few more marshmallows, Sammy seemed much happier. They talked for a long time, and Jimmy found Sammy to be completely different from the quiet person he had seen at the press conference in Cairo. The boy he shared a tent with now was loud, energetic, and funny.

Before long the efforts of the day began to catch up with the boys. They decided to settle down for the night. Jimmy hopped into his sleeping bag and curled up on Maverick's back seat.

"Good night, Sammy," he called out.

"Good night, Jimmy. Sleep well."

"Good night, Maximus," said Jimmy.

"*Tisbah ala kheir!*" called the robot.

"He says good night," translated Maverick.

"Good night, Maverick."

"Night! Er . . . Jimmy?"

"Yes, Maverick?" Jimmy yawned.

"Could you throw a couple more logs on the fire? It's pretty dark now. I wouldn't want you to get too cold and —"

Jimmy grinned. "Maverick, do you want the fire to keep snakes away?"

There was a long, embarrassed silence before Maverick spoke again. "Yes, please."

Jimmy put more wood on the fire. Then he climbed back into Maverick and fell asleep, the sounds of the rain forest all around them.

★ ★ ★

After a few hours of sleep, Jimmy was woken by bright sunlight streaming through Maverick's windows. He rubbed his eyes and sat up. Outside the jungle was waking up too. Birds were singing their morning songs, small animals were collecting their breakfast, and the monkeys were howling a wake-up call. It was a clear and bright morning, and Jimmy felt refreshed and ready for anything.

"Morning, Jimmy!" said Maverick energetically. "It's a new day, and that means only one thing!"

"We've got some racing to do!" said Jimmy, pumped up with energy. He leaped out of his sleeping bag and out into the jungle. Sammy was just getting out of Maximus, stretching and yawning.

"Good morning!" said Jimmy. "Did you sleep well?"

"Yes, thank you," Sammy replied.

Jimmy and Sammy cleaned up their camp and ate breakfast. Then they arranged the start time for the next leg of the race with the Robot Races officials through the Cabcom.

Because Maverick and Maximus had come off the official track in an accident, they had to make their way directly to the official track first. Then they had to go through the luxury camp where everyone else had slept and carry on with the race from there. They had more ground to cover than the other racers, but all they could do was try their best.

Grandpa popped up on the screen after the officials went away. "Jimmy? Did you have a good night?"

"Yeah, sort of," said Jimmy. It had been surprisingly fun after such a crazy day.

"Omar is going insane over here. He says he can't contact Samir."

"Oh, yeah. Tell him the Cabcom was damaged in the accident," said Jimmy. He looked over to Sammy, who grinned.

Then suddenly a ten-second countdown appeared on Jimmy's Cabcom to start the second leg of the race.

"Maverick and Maximus, are you ready?" said the voice of Joshua Johnson, the Robot Coordinator, over the speakers.

"Born ready!" said Maverick.

"Then you are good to go in five . . ."

Maverick revved his engine.

"Four . . ."

Maximus's turbo rotors spun, readying themselves.

"Three . . ."

Jimmy looked over and gave a good-luck nod to Sammy.

"Two . . ."

Sammy gave a salute back and turned his attention to the race.

"One! Go, go, GO!" shouted Joshua Johnson.

In a flurry of leaves and mud, Maverick was off! To Jimmy's surprise, Maximus was hot on their tail, a smiling Sammy at the controls. It looked like Jimmy was right. Without his dad yelling at him, Sammy was a great racer. Sammy was taking corners at high speed and throwing Maximus around the track in daring moves that his father would never approve of. He was doing great and having the time of his life!

They found their way back onto the official track. Within minutes, both robots were zooming into the main camp. Grandpa was waiting and waved at Jimmy to pull in.

The rest of the teams had had all night to patch, repair, reprogram, and refuel their robot. But for Grandpa, it was a race against the clock. As Maverick pulled in, race officials stood over him with a stopwatch and clipboard in their hands. Joshua Johnson stood with them.

"Wow! You've been through a lot, haven't you?" said Grandpa as he saw the state of Maverick, but there was no time to chat. He placed his steaming mug of tea on top of Maverick's roof and got to work.

Grandpa whizzed around the car, refueling and checking tires. The other crews, which were made up of professionals in white overalls, watched Grandpa as he zipped around the robot. He stuck a fuel nozzle in the side of the car, quickly reinflated the tires, and threw a banana into the driver's seat.

Grandpa wrenched off the broken fender and kicked a dented side panel until it popped out. He then squirted a bottle of water over the windshield to clean it. He banged the roof to show he was finished. He just had time to pull the fuel nozzle out and grab his mug of tea before Jimmy sped away.

Jimmy glanced in his mirror as he tore away. He could see Grandpa fall into a nearby chair, exhausted. Sammy's pit crew was still working on Maximus.

"Good work, Grandpa!" Jimmy laughed.

Driving away from the pit, the jungle closed in around the track again. Up ahead, Jimmy could see the trees growing thicker. The tree canopies made everything extra dark. Jimmy wasn't sure he would be able to pick out the right way to go.

"Hey, Maverick, you remember Horace said he had a better navigation system than you? Well, I think it's time to put it to the test."

"Received and understood, Jimmy!" said the chirpy robot. "Calculating route now."

There was a series of blips and beeps. Then a map popped up on the screen, a red line indicating the best route to take.

"This will guide us through this thick forest. Hold on tight, pay attention, and I'll talk you through the curves," said Maverick. "If you follow what I say exactly, we can do this at top speed."

"Okay," said Jimmy, slightly nervous. "Let's do it!"

He focused, tightening his grip on the steering wheel and listening for Maverick's instructions. As the trees closed in on him, he instinctively braked.

"No, maintain your speed!" said Maverick, and Jimmy put his foot back on the accelerator. "Turn thirty degrees left now!"

Jimmy did so, narrowly missing a giant tree that must have been there for hundreds of years.

Jimmy wanted to shut his eyes, but then he'd definitely crash. Maverick kept shouting instructions. Jimmy followed them perfectly, trusting the robot's directions and his own reactions to get them through. They were still on the official track, which was marked by glowing markers on trees and posts. However, Maverick was taking a risky route, clinging to the edge of the track to keep the speed up, and flying over bumps in the road rather than going around them.

"Left! Right! Forty-five degrees west! Hairpin bend!" yelled Maverick, branches whizzing past them, leaves and insects splatting against the windshield.

Jimmy braced himself as he came to the tight curve. He threw the steering wheel to the left and right, moving through the glowing posts. He came out of the obstacle, and Maverick shouted at him once more as they headed into a sharp turn that Jimmy hadn't noticed.

"Eeek!" said Jimmy as they just missed a huge tree. He held his breath as they skimmed over the top of a large, deep puddle. He didn't speak until they were clear of the trees and back onto a normal mud track.

Jimmy breathed a sigh of relief that they had made it through. Then he concentrated on the route ahead. They turned a corner and saw the other competitors right in front of them.

"We've caught up!" said Jimmy. "If we can get in front of this group, we could still win!"

"That's the spirit!" cheered Maverick.

Jimmy was excited at the thought of whizzing past Horace, but his smile faded slightly when he saw why the other robots had slowed down. The track took them over the top of an area that looked like a yellow lake.

"Quicksand!" he gasped. The other robots were being careful. They knew that if they slipped off the track, they would sink like stones. Then they would be out of the race for good.

Missy and Monster was at the back of the group, following the others down a safe route at the center of the track.

"Get out of the way!" said Maverick. Jimmy steered them to the left, and tried to push past Monster, but Missy must have seen them coming. She steered left too, blocking the way. Jimmy immediately steered right, trying to overtake on the other side, but Monster followed, blocking the way past again.

"Well, if that's the way you want to play it . . ." muttered Jimmy. He looked directly ahead and quickly guessed the height of the monster truck in front of him. "We can just make it!"

"Make what?" said Maverick.

"If we can't go around her, we'll have to go under," Jimmy replied. And with that he hit a button on the steering wheel. There was a whirring noise, and Maverick's suspension lowered, making the whole car hunch down lower to the road. Jimmy floored the accelerator and powered right under Monster. They passed huge wheels on either side. The sound was deafening, and the vibration from the enormous engine made Jimmy's teeth chatter.

But then they sped between the front tires of Monster and back into the daylight and into fourth place! Just ahead of them was Lightning.

"Let's see if we can get past Her Highness!" said Jimmy. He put on a burst of speed and was almost touching the back of Kako's robobike. This race was intense!

"Here we go!" he said. He kept his speed and waved at Kako. She smiled back, looking over at him. Suddenly the track came to a sharp turn.

Kako had been caught off guard and had to slow down to go around it safely. Jimmy had seen the curve ahead, and he was ready. He roared through it, keeping his speed the same and overtaking Lightning.

"That's my boy," came Grandpa's voice over the Cabcom.

"Thanks, Grandpa. Maverick, how far ahead is the next racer?"

"Just under half a mile, Jimmy. You should be able to see Dug at the end of this straightaway."

Sure enough Jimmy caught a glimpse of Chip's huge racer up ahead. He knew that Dug would be even trickier to pass than the last two.

"Just under fifteen miles to go. That's not much racing time, Jimmy. If we want to beat Smelly Pelly, we'll need to make this pass double quick."

"I know, I know. We never make things easy for ourselves, do we?" Jimmy said.

Jimmy moved Maverick to the far right of the track as he sped up toward the rear bumper of the giant digger. As he expected, Chip blocked the way. Jimmy swerved to the left, but was blocked again. Then he tried to pass to the right once more. Again he was blocked.

Now I've got you where I want you, Jimmy thought. He pulled the steering wheel to the left again, but only for a second. When Dug moved to block the way on the left, Jimmy quickly whipped the steering wheel to the right and overtook in the large space that the digger had left open. Maverick's engine roared, and they zipped by an astonished Chip.

"Ha ha!" laughed Maverick. "Nice move!"

At that moment, Horace's sneering face appeared on the Cabcom.

"Been having fun with Maverick, Jimmy? Now that you've finished messing around with the amateurs, I'll show you how us pros do it."

Jimmy and Maverick were in second place now, close enough to see Zoom's shiny black bodywork in front. Jimmy accelerated and pulled alongside Zoom.

Horace glanced at them from his cab. "Back again, Jimmy? You never learn, do you?"

Maverick was about to overtake, when the familiar jets of red-hot flames shot out from Zoom's wheels.

"Yowzer!" screamed Maverick. He pulled to the side but kept his speed. He had singed the outside of his tires. Jimmy could smell the burning rubber.

Horace laughed as he pressed the button again, and more flames shot out. It forced Maverick to the very edge of the track, closer and closer to the huge pool of quicksand on his left. His tires screeched as they rubbed against the edge of the track. Jimmy looked and saw the quicksand waiting to grab hold of him and pull him down into its depths.

"No way, Horace! Not again!" shouted Jimmy.

CHAPTER 14
RACE TO THE FINISH

Jimmy's face turned red with anger. He gritted his teeth and roughly slammed the steering wheel with a fist.

"Ow! Watch it!" said Maverick.

Jimmy didn't say anything. He was so mad that for a moment he thought about simply ramming into Zoom. "No," he said to himself quickly. "That's how he'd race. It's not my style."

Suddenly the roar of Dug's engine was upon them. As the track widened, Chip took the opportunity to steer the digger robot alongside the other two. In their efforts to outdo each other, Jimmy and Horace had given Chip a chance to catch up.

Dug moved between Maverick and Zoom. While the flames from Zoom's wheels had burned the rubber on Maverick's tires, they had no effect on Dug's thick tractor-like tires. Chip glanced over at Jimmy, giving a smile before his face appeared on the Cabcom, next to Horace's.

"Hey, guys! Mind if I join the party?" he said. "This one's for you, Horace!" He pressed a button on his dashboard, and there was an explosion of smoke from Dug's rear. The smoke billowed out, creating a cloud of thick fog around Zoom and Horace, making it impossible for them to see.

Horace yelled out in terror as Zoom veered wildly.

Jimmy smiled. After Horace had pushed Chip and Dug over the canyon in the last race, they deserved that. Jimmy could hear Horace panicking over the Cabcom.

"Aaaargh! Activate the laser guidance system!" Horace squealed.

A grid of lasers shot out from Zoom's nose, but the smoke was so thick that they couldn't cut through it. A series of confused bleeps came from Zoom, and the computer-assisted steering program lost its way. Zoom hit the edge of the track, and the engine roared as his wheels spun madly. The sleek black robot launched over the edge, sliding down into the quicksand with a final splosh!

"Aaagh! Deploy emergency lifesaving apparatus!" yelled Horace to Zoom.

"Lifesaving apparatus is situated below the pilot's seat," said the cool, calm tones of Zoom. After a moment of fumbling below him, Horace came back on the screen.

"Rope? Rope? Is that the best you can do? I want my money back from NASA!"

"Uh — Jimmy?" called Maverick. "QUICKSAND, DEAD AHEAD!"

"Uh-oh," said Jimmy as he saw what Maverick was talking about. In front of them the road was sank into the lake of quicksand. The track ended and picked up again about a hundred yards later, leaving no other way to finish the race. And Maverick was just seconds away from the yellow pool of sandy sludge.

"Slow down!" yelled Maverick.

Jimmy glanced at the rest of the racers behind him and quickly hatched a plan. "No! Quick, Maverick, release the EFD!"

"Pardon?"

"Activate the Emergency Floatation Device!"

"The what?"

Jimmy sighed. "The rubber dinghy! Inflate the dinghy, quick!" he shouted.

"Oh, right!" said Maverick. "Why didn't you say so?"

With a noise like a hundred whoopee cushions, a rubber skirt unfurled around Maverick. Then a canister of compressed air inflated the device within seconds. "Jimmy? Did you know you're speeding up?" said Maverick's worried voice.

"Yup," smiled Jimmy.

"We're going to hit the quicksand at full speed! Slow down!"

Jimmy kept his foot on the pedal and patted Maverick's steering wheel. "It's okay. I know what I'm doing. I think . . ."

They raced along the track to where it sank into the sand and hit the quicksand with a loud slosh! But instead of sinking, Maverick glided across the pool as the dinghy kept them from sinking into the deadly gloop. It was almost peaceful, sliding across the sand. The engine was quiet. Jimmy just had to wait to hit the track on the other side.

He looked behind him and found the rest of the competitors squealing to a stop, unable to make the jump to the other side. Everyone, that is, except Sammy and Maximus, whose hovercraft cushion was perfect for this sort of situation. They headed onto the quicksand without a moment's hesitation and moved along just as easily as they did on the road.

Jimmy had timed his sail across the quicksand perfectly. He was just losing speed when the road appeared again. He was able to drive off onto the path with no problems.

"That was so lucky!" said Maverick.

"Nah!" Jimmy chuckled. "It was exactly how I planned it."

They were in first place! Jimmy looked back to see Maximus emerging from the quicksand and coming at them fast. He could also just make out the rest of the competitors on the other side. There was no time to see how they were doing, because Maximus was right behind them.

"Let's go, go, go!" said Jimmy.

However friendly Sammy and Jimmy had become, Jimmy knew that their friendship would have to be put aside until they crossed the finish line. They were true robot racers, and neither was prepared to give an inch. Maximus pulled alongside Maverick.

"How far until the finish line?" shouted Jimmy above the noise of the straining engine. He could barely hear himself yell.

"Not far!" said Maverick. "Keep your eye on the road, though. We've got a few more corners to navigate."

The first corner came almost immediately. Jimmy skidded around it in a high gear. Maximus was right by his side, the hovercraft's back end drifting out as he made the turn. They were just inches apart.

Jimmy glanced over to see Sammy hunched over his controls, concentrating on the race. Next came a tight corner, which the two robots raced around as fast as their drivers dared.

Then the finish line came into sight. Jimmy could see the crowds at the finish line now, roaring their support. It was clear that Sammy wasn't going to give up on first place, and neither was Jimmy!

"If only we still had our nitro-blasters," muttered Jimmy. "Come on, Maverick, just a bit faster!"

"This is all we've got!" the robot shot back. "It's going to be tight!"

Jimmy held his breath. Time seemed to slow down for the last few seconds of the race. He was aware of the crowds in the stand, waving their flags in slow motion. He could see the journalists waiting up ahead. He saw Sammy beside him, gripping the wheel tightly as he raced toward the finish line. The sound seemed to drop away. All Jimmy could hear was the cheers of the fans and the whir of the engine.

Maverick and Maximus flew past the finish line and Lord Leadpipe, who was waving the checkered flag. It was several seconds before Jimmy let himself breathe again. The cameras around the grandstand flashed. The sound returned to normal as the crowd let out an almighty cheer. It was the loudest thing Jimmy had ever heard.

Maverick and Maximus finally slowed to a stop. Jimmy leaped out onto the track, where Sammy was already waiting, his helmet in his hands. They looked around.

"Who won?" the boys said together, but the race officials just shrugged at them. No one knew who had crossed the line first.

An electronic leader board by the side of the stands flashed, and Jimmy and Sammy looked over.

"Seeking official race results," said a computer voice.

Jimmy felt too nervous to talk. The crowd was silent.

"Photo evidence inconclusive," said the computer again. "No winner was identified. Now seeking results from advanced laser finish line technology."

Jimmy was willing the computer to come up with the right result as he focused on the leader board.

"The results have now been found," said the computer finally.

"And?" muttered Sammy.

"And?" whispered Jimmy.

There was one more moment before the display changed. Suddenly the crowd erupted.

"First place — a tie! Jimmy and Maverick and Sammy and Maximus!"

Sammy and Jimmy stared at each other in disbelief. The photo finish on the screen confirmed it. They had crossed at exactly the same time!

A message ran over the bottom of the screen:

For the first time in Robot Races history a tie has been awarded for the title of first place. Well done, Jimmy and Sammy!

Jimmy ran to Sammy and shook his hand. The Egyptian smiled and pulled him into a great big bear hug. They heard the crowd chanting their names.

"Sam-my! Jim-my! Sam-my! Jim-my!"

"I think they're calling for you!" said Jimmy.

"I think they want both of us!" corrected Sammy.

They both ran over to the grandstand and waved to the crowd.

The other racers came in past the finish line and slowed to a stop. Chip came in next, followed by Missy and Monster, who were covered in sand. Kako came in fifth and did not look happy. The leader board flashed up the results. The last team on the screen was Horace and Zoom, with a red DNF next to their names.

"Horace and Zoom didn't finish?" said Jimmy. "Just when I thought my day couldn't get any better."

It was over ten minutes before the safetybots dragged in a sandy-looking Zoom and Horace. Jimmy peered into Zoom's cockpit and noticed it looked a little bare.

"Where's the laser guidance system you added?" Jimmy asked with a smile on his face.

"If you must know, it fell off and sank in the quicksand," spat Horace. "And I intend to complain to Lord Leadpipe about the unsafe track and deadly traps, not to mention the sabotage! The whole race should be discounted!"

His whining trailed off as the safetybots moved on, taking Zoom off to the pits to be fixed and cleaned out. Jimmy started to walk away toward the pit.

"Hey!" said a voice behind him. "Where do you think you're going?"

It was Joshua Johnson, with a big smile on his face. He grabbed Jimmy and led him and Sammy over to a small stage, where they were both pushed onto the top of the winner's podium. It had only been built for one winner, but Jimmy and Sammy both squeezed on happily.

The officials gave them both a giant bottle of sparkling lemonade. Jimmy grinned at Sammy and knew exactly what to do. He popped the cork from the top of his bottle and started shaking it up. Sammy copied him, and then both boys sprayed the fizzy drink everywhere! The crowd cheered as they turned the bottles on the fans and journalists who were snapping their photos.

With the last bit left in his bottle, Jimmy hopped down from the podium and approached his racer.

"You look a bit dirty, Maverick," he said mischievously.

"Don't you dare!" shouted the robot, but Jimmy had already shaken the bottle again. The lemonade fizzed over the top and sprayed over Maverick's hood, the robot protesting the whole time. Joshua Johnson grabbed them again for more photos on the podium before he would allow them to leave.

Jimmy could hardly hear himself think with the crowds shouting his name, and he didn't even notice Grandpa running toward him.

"That's my boy!" laughed Grandpa, his wiry arms gripping Jimmy tightly.

Jimmy looked over and saw the stern face of Omar Bahur approaching, a scowl on his face as usual. He faced Sammy and extended a hand for a very business-like handshake. Sammy gave his hand too, and looked shocked when his father broke out into a grin and gathered him up into a bear hug instead.

"Samir, my child, you were extraordinary! Your first Robot Races win! A father has never been so proud!"

Sammy smiled, looking confused and embarrassed by his father's unusual behavior.

"You must forgive me. I know how much of a bully I have been. I must be a better father in the future. You must know that I am very proud of you."

"I hope so," muttered Grandpa under his breath.

"You are remarkable! Quick-thinking and brave!" continued Omar. "Such an intelligent boy!"

"Yes. I must get it from Mother," Sammy joked.

"I'd still be at the bottom of a hole if it weren't for Sammy," said Jimmy. They were about to shake hands for the cameras when two men wearing green suits and smelling slightly of cabbage barged in and took Grandpa and Jimmy off to one side. A photographer approached, snapping pictures.

"Jimmy, it's a pleasure to meet you at last!" said the first man, shaking his hand. "I'm Felix Crump from That's Shallot! This is my business partner, Jasper Sprout. I trust our little gift came in handy?"

A TV camera was now being pushed into Jimmy's face. "Um . . . yes. The Carrot Vision was a lifesaver," said Jimmy, a bit taken aback by the two strange men.

"Of course!" Felix Crump grinned at the camera. "Our carrots are packed full of goodness and really do help you see in the dark!" he said. "And that's why we're giving you a lifetime supply of carrots! What do you say to that, Jimmy?"

"Uh . . ."

"Overjoyed, you say? You're welcome! And it's all thanks to That's Shallot! Your cheaper way to five a day!"

Grandpa managed to pull Jimmy away. "How are you feeling, Jimmy?" he said.

"A little overwhelmed, to be honest. I just can't believe everything that is happening," Jimmy said.

"Get used to it, boy! This is what it's like to be a winner!" Grandpa smiled and pointed up to the big screen, which now showed the results of the two races overall.

Jimmy felt like he was in a bizarre dream as the announcer read the results. The crowd cheered as each name was mentioned. They came to the top of the leader board.

"And let's hear it for Jimmy Roberts and his robot Maverick as they climb to the top of the leader board. First place! Great job!"

The crowd cheered and screamed his name as Felix and Jasper from That's Shallot! hoisted him onto their shoulders in celebration.

"Yes," said Jimmy to himself. "I could get used to this . . ."

CHAPTER 15
CONGRATS TO THE WINNER!

It was a long time before the crowds calmed down, and even longer before the journalists and TV crews had stopped shouting out questions.

"How does it feel to share first place?"

"What's the secret to a good race?"

"Have you got anything you can tell the folks back home?"

Jimmy didn't know which to answer first, but luckily he saw that someone was coming to take control of the situation. Through the crowd of cameras and the tangle of wires, came a familiar face.

Bet Bristle from Robo TV battled her way through the other journalists, knocking them out of the way with her elbows. "Well done, boys!" she said with a smile that silenced the rest of the journalists. "Tell me, we lost you on the tracking system for a while yesterday. Neither of your teams could contact you. What happened?"

Jimmy took the lead in the interview. He explained about their daring adventure.

Bet looked exhausted at the end of the tale. She turned to Sammy. "Samir," she said, "you've been typically quiet throughout all of this. How did you cope with this ordeal?"

Sammy looked at the crowd. He did not answer right away. Instead, he took a pair of sunglasses out of his coat pocket and put them on.

He shrugged. "I wasn't frightened at all," he said.

Bet tried to get more out of him, but he refused to answer any more questions. Jimmy raised an eyebrow at his new friend. When the journalists had moved on to talk to the other competitors, Sammy looked over the top of his shades and smiled.

"I have an image to think of," he said. "It might be fun to be the cool, silent guy! Time to see all of my fans."

Jimmy shook his head in disbelief as Sammy walked off to sign some autographs.

With the attention of the world finally off him, Jimmy was about to make his way to see how Grandpa and Maverick were doing when he heard a voice call out, "Our young winner!" It was Lord Leadpipe, his monocle glinting in the light of the sunshine. "Congratulations, Master Roberts. Good race, eh? You're turning into quite the champion!"

"Thank you." Jimmy felt his cheeks turning bright red.

"Let's see if this pack of hungry photographers would like a photo of me with the winners, hmm?" said Lord Leadpipe with a chuckle. He started to lead them toward the press pit, where some paparazzi turned and began to snap away at them.

Jimmy felt a hand clamp down on his shoulder, stopping him.

"No more photographs, Ludwick," said Grandpa, appearing by his side. "The boy's tired."

Leadpipe seemed startled by Grandpa's sudden appearance. "Well, quite. I suppose you have a lot of debriefing to go through. Team talks, as it were."

Grandpa nodded, fixing Lord Leadpipe with a silent stare. Only when Leadpipe broke the stare and turned around to leave did Grandpa say anything.

"That's the thing with Jimmy and me," he said. "We are a team. We're loyal, and we stick together."

Lord Leadpipe turned on his heel to face Grandpa again, but before he could say anything in response, someone shouted, "There he is!"

Jimmy turned to see Mr. Pelly marching up to Leadpipe, looking like he was going to explode with anger. Horace trailed after his dad, covered in mud and sand.

"Ludwick! I want a word with you about track safety! My boy could have been killed!" he said. "And what's worse is that my robot is now ruined! There's sand everywhere!"

Lord Leadpipe waved his hand. "Pelly, you'll have to take this up with the track stewards," he said dismissively. "I have a very important announcement to make!"

He took to the stage in the center of the race compound to the sound of a cheering crowd. His face appeared everywhere at once, on every TV screen, including two huge ones the size of billboards. It was even projected onto the entire side of the Leadpipe Industries airship, which hovered high above their heads.

"Robot Races fans!" boomed Lord Leadpipe. "Our racers have defeated the Rain Forest Rampage, but there are tougher tasks yet to come. I can tell you that the next race will be enthralling, exciting, and of course, unexpected. And I will be introducing a very special twist!"

The crowd was silent.

"But that, my friends, is all I will say for now." Lord Leadpipe flashed a grin at the TV cameras, then pointed his special gold-tipped walking cane at the sky. He pressed a button on the handle, and crackling electricity shot from it into the clouds above, where fireworks flashed and banged, lighting the jungle up with bright reds and yellows.

As the familiar sound of the Robot Races theme tune kicked in and the audience clapped along to the beat, Lord Leadpipe turned back to the TV cameras. "Stay tuned for the next installment of the engine-revving, rough-and-ready, rip-roaring Robot Races, coming soon!"

"I wonder what's he got up his sleeve this time?" said Grandpa.

"Well, whatever it is, we'll be ready for it!" said Jimmy.

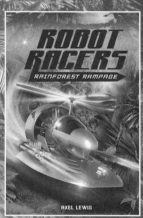